SUTTER CANE

IN THE MOUTH OF MADNESS

ARCANE PUBLISHING

Copyright © 2025 Michael De Luca.
All Rights Reserved.

This novelization is based on the original screenplay of *In The Mouth of Madness* written by Michael De Luca. Novelization rights licensed by Echo On Publications under WGA separated rights.

In The Mouth of Madness and all related characters and elements are trademarks of and © New Line Productions, Inc. a division of Warner Bros. All rights in the original motion picture are owned by New Line Productions, Inc. a division of Warner Bros, and are used with permission where applicable.

The characters and events contained in these pages are fictitious. Any similarity to real persons, living, dead, or undead, is purely coincidental and not intended by the author.

No part of this book may be reproduced in any form or by any electronic or mechanical means, including information storage and retrieval systems, without permission in writing from the publisher, except by a reviewer who may quote brief passages in a review.

ISBN 978-1-916582-81-1 (*ebook*)
ISBN 978-1-916582-89-7 (*Trade paperback*)
ISBN 978-1-916582-82-8 (*hardcover*)

echohorror.com

Contents

Prologue	1
Chapter 1	5
Chapter 2	39
Chapter 3	61
Chapter 4	89
Chapter 5	109
Chapter 6	133
Chapter 7	157
Chapter 8	189
Chapter 9	219
The Final Word	251
Prologue from The Feeding	255

Prologue

The printing press was a beast of engineering. An unrelenting, mechanical colossus that had transcended the simplicity of its origins. The invention of the Gutenberg press, conceived half a millennium ago, had been seized, reshaped, and forcibly evolved into what was now a juggernaut of automation.

Gears churned and belts whirred as mechanical arms slammed together in a furious yet flawless synchronization. From within the vast structure, the machine roared with deafening rhythms. Beautifully chaotic and hypnotic as it chugged, hissed, and clattered its way through its singular, powerful purpose.

Printing plates, wet with ink, were set into place as endless sheets of paper sped through the wide rollers, drawn in like an unending, sacrificial offering. One after another, the blank reams were drawn into its metal maw, vanishing beneath a blur of movement. As the impression cylinder struck, it held each sheet against the inked plates, transferring crisp, black lettering in an instant. These stained pages were then flipped over and sent through this process once more, as the next collection of words were branded onto their reverse.

The uncut sheets soon fed through the conveyor belts, where spinning blades sliced through them with precision, carving them into smaller pages. The pages were then gathered, collated, and stacked before surging forward into the next unit. Their edges were perfectly aligned before meeting the binder.

A rhythmic hiss followed as a wave of molten adhesive was applied to each paper block's spine. The next set of rollers guided each one into the trimming machine, where the excess paper was sheared away, leaving each with a clean and sharp edge. The books were nearly complete. Their forms were finally taking shape. Only their covers remained. Their skin.

From another side of the press, the covers soon emerged, still warm from the heat of the machinery that had created them. They came in a relentless tide, dozens upon dozens of identical, soon-to-be-cut images, piled in stacks, waiting to be attached.

The artwork upon them was unmistakable, as striking as the author's five previous works—*my works*. It displayed a black church silhouetted against a storm-choked sky. A vast, monstrous creature lurked behind it, clawed limbs grasping around its steeple. The thing stared outward, its gaze locked with the reader, its other claw lifted high, ready to strike. Across the top, embossed in bold, unignorable lettering, was my name: *Sutter Cane*. Below that, the title of the tale: *The Hobb's End Horror*.

This was to be the second-to-last book I would ever write, that I *could* ever write. The penultimate tale before the end.

The covers were fed into the next great automaton. They were sliced, applied, and fused to their waiting bodies. When complete, they were flipped onto the final conveyor belt, face down as they emerged from the press, ready to be boxed.

Each cover's reverse bore the same vague synopsis I had crafted. The standard teaser to lure in eager eyes. But it was not those words that mattered. It was what was written beneath that was important. For this was the first time the next words had ever been printed. The first time they had been seen in that formation.

This cover was the herald. It was a portent of something dark and inevitable.

Beneath the bold *Coming Soon from Sutter Cane* banner, there they were. The words of my prologue to the end: *In the Mouth of Madness*.

Again and again, the machine repeated the message, spitting out book after book, as if printing the name onto the very fabric of reality.

Which it very much was.

No one could have foretold what was to come. People would just see the title and look forward to another scary story yet to be published. They would not realize, *you* would not realize, that there was never going to be any choice.

You were always going to read this book.

You just didn't know it then.

Chapter One

The rain came down in torrents, hard and cold, hammering the ambulance like it owed the sky money. Not the romantic kind. This was old-world, biblical rain that sounded more like a brutal punishment. A thunder-booming, building-rattling storm that had fury toward everything it hit.

The driveway up the hill was a smeared mass of darkness and flashbulb lightning. The ambulance's headlights shone as pale tunnels through the darkness, through the continuous curtain of water, as it screamed its way past the entrance sign.

Through the windscreen, a blur of rusted lettering on wet stone read: *New York State Institute for the Criminally Insane.*

Inside, strapped to a gurney, wrapped in a strait-jacket and sealed behind a leather and steel muzzle, a man screamed up a storm of his own.

Sutter Cane

"Get me the fuck out of here!" he yelled for the hundredth time, still pleading that it was a mistake that he was even here. A plea the orderlies in front had heard a hundred times on their way to the institute. By now, the man's voice was raw, his vocal cords shredded from screaming. His eyes were bulging with fear and desperation, as he hoped someone would not just hear him, but help him.

The sound of his angry and begging cries barely escaped the padded cab, muffled by restraints, and under the blaring siren that wailed upon the roof.

The orderlies, both built like linebackers, were emotionally unavailable to this patient. They sat in silence in the front seats, stoic, disinterested. When they first started their jobs, it had been quite different, they worried about the soon-to-be-inmates. But now, after all they had seen, they didn't get paid nearly enough to care.

The man in back continued to thrash on the gurney, even though he knew his screams were being ignored. He wrenched his body left and right, up and down, hoping for the restraints to give way, but they were too thick, too strong. All his struggle did was make the straps dig into his chest, wrists, and shoulders. It was futile, and sore.

Eventually realizing this, the man slumped back against the pillow, exhausted. Covered in a sheen of sweat, half from the exertion, half from panic. His hair clung to his forehead in damp strands as he grumbled to himself that he even got in this situation in the first place.

Maybe the axe was a step too far? He thought. *No. It was needed.*

As the lightning flashed outside, coupled with an immediate bellowing of thunder, the man's anger soon abated. His expression fell as he took a deep, nervous breath inward, realizing that he was almost there.

Nurse Margaret had been the night shift supervisor long enough to stop her from wondering why things got worse after dark. Especially in a facility like this one. There was a rhythm to the madness within these walls, and the nighttime just amplified that. It didn't matter that all the inmates in the maximum-security ward were rowdy and awake all day, they were just that much more active at night. And on a full moon? They were wild. Like tonight.

The reception desk sat at the dimly lit entrance to the ward, a small island in the wide corridor before the long row of padded cells stretched through corridors behind it. She ignored the shouts and screams coming from them and just focused on her work, as much as she was able. Hunched over a clipboard, she scanned the transfer report, as a heavy, persistent pain throbbed in her skull. A headache that had taken root behind her eyes since she had woken up, and it hadn't abated since. Not even the constant stream of nicotine or caffeine had helped. Not that it ever would. They at least kept her awake.

It was 3 a.m. and her brain felt waterlogged. Medical jargon at this hour was the devil's crossword puzzle anyway, but in her pained fog, she was barely taking in any words on the paper. She knew the expected patient's name, but no matter how many times she read his medical history, she could not retain that information.

Then she heard it.

Beyond the cries from the ward. A sound. Muffled, at first.

One voice. A man. An *angry* man.

Getting louder. Nearer.

Screaming like bloody murder.

The yells that followed were so loud, that it should have surprised her like a slap. But she had been here hundreds of times. Instead, she just grimaced.

"Great," she said. "Another loud one."

On the ward, she had enough 'screamers', as she not-so-lovingly called them. And getting another would do just one thing... Make her headache worse.

The double doors to her left swung open, banging against the wall, as figures staggered into view. The two large orderlies, wearing rain-soaked trench coats, hauled between them the straight-jacketed man. His body bucked and twisted as he tried to rip himself free.

Nurse Margaret sighed loudly as she put the clipboard down and stared, as the orderlies struggled, dragging the man across the tiled floor.

Still wearing a leather-strapped muzzle, the man was incensed. Though his mouth could not be seen, his eyes could. Wild, bloodshot and carrying dark bags.

The nurse watched as he was dragged closer. *Here's a man who looks exactly how I feel*, she thought.

One of the orderlies held up a manila folder, stealing her attention.

"Another one for ya," he said.

"Can you confirm the name?" she asked with a sigh.

"Trent, John J.," the orderly grunted, keeping as firm a grip on the man's arm as possible. "He's—"

The sentence was cut short as Trent, with a loud grunt, kicked backward. His bare foot connected solidly and heavily with the orderly's groin. The man doubled over with a yelp, releasing his grip, as the folder fell to the floor beside him.

"Where you going, fucko?" the second orderly snapped. Without hesitation, his arm flew out across Trent's neck like a steel bar, stopping him as he turned to flee. The orderly grabbed him by the hair and slammed his head against the desk. The crack echoed down the corridor. A sound that made the inmates in the ward yell from their cells with glee. Yells like from a zoo.

Trent collapsed onto the floor in a moaning heap, blood dripping from a new gash on his forehead. He groaned a low gurgle, then spat a mouthful of blood through the muzzle and onto the tiled floor below him.

The downed orderly, breathing hard, staggered to his feet as he steadied himself on the edge of the desk. Retrieving the dropped folder, he slid it across to Nurse Margaret.

"Trent, John J," he repeated, this time in a wheeze.

None of this had fazed the nurse. She stared at the folder then the orderly, then the man on the floor.

"Take him to Number Nine," she said, disinterested, handing them a large set of keys on a big keyring. A set that looked more at home in a dungeon than a medical facility.

The dark corridor to Cell Nine snaked off from the reception desk. Only lit at this time of night by dull orange bulbs, which only served enough illumination to see where you needed to go.

Down here were Cells One through Ten. All holding grounds for new arrivals. These recent inmates were usually the more feral. The wild-eyed and the volatile. The ones who wanted out. The ones not resigned to their fate yet. This is where they were kept until the medication could take hold, until the edge of their mania could wear off... or at least reached some kind of equilibrium. But for maximum-security inmates, that equilibrium was just as loud, erratic, and dangerous.

In The Mouth of Madness

As the orderlies dragged Trent down the corridor, he had no strength left to fight. His feet dragged behind him as his arms were gripped between the men.

At first, the corridor of the ward reeked of bleach. A sharp, sterile, almost reassuring smell that you'd expect in a clinical environment. But the longer anyone lingered, the more it became clear that the acrid sting wasn't cleanliness, it was just a mask. Beneath it festered the real scent. A rancid stew of shit, piss, sweat and despair. Something you felt in the back of your throat. The stench of past inmates, soaked into the walls, that no dousing of chemicals could truly remove. It was a smell that was caked into the bare concrete itself.

Cell Nine was the second to last room on the row. As they approached, the orderly that had been kicked still grimaced in pain.

"You got the key?" he asked.

The other orderly fumbled in his pocket and pulled out the large keyring.

Metal clinked and rattled as he found the right one and slid it into the lock.

The cell door soon creaked open.

Four padded walls, yellowed by age and other less sanitary things, surrounded a single bare mattress on the floor, and above, a dangling bare lightbulb buzzed loudly.

As his muzzle was removed, Trent's bravado sank, and his panic set in, seeing the reality of where he was.

"No," he mumbled in a rising panic, as he started to pull his arms free. "No, no, no, no, no, no—"

"Uh-oh," the pained orderly said. "he's back for another round."

"Get him in," said the other.

Trent screamed as they shoved him. He twisted, panicked, turned and clawed at the padded door frame, trying to keep a grip, to stop them from putting him in here.

"No!" he bellowed. "Not me! It's not me! Please! *Listen!*"

But he had no chance. Both men surged forward, barging him in the back, pushing him over the threshold. As he did, part of the padded door frame came off in his grip.

"You can't put me in here," he screamed again. *"You don't know what it is!"*

The cell door soon slammed shut with a metallic bang, trapping Trent inside.

For a moment, as the orderlies looked through the small, windowed slot in the door, nothing could be seen or heard, and there was only silence from the man.

With wild eyes and sweat dripping down his face, Trent appeared at the glass, pressing his face into the bars.

The orderlies smirked and walked away. Leaving him locked in Cell Nine.

In The Mouth of Madness

"Wait! Hey!" Trent shrieked. "I'm sorry about the balls! It was a lucky shot!"

The orderlies disappeared down the corridor and past the reception desk, nodding to Nurse Margaret as if everything here was perfectly normal.

"I'm not insane!" Trent screamed from far behind them, *"I'm not fucking insane!"*

And, like an unhinged chorus, other voices joined in with Trent's protestation. From the cells along each corridor that had heard. A torrent of mania ensued.

"Me neither!"

"He's as sane as I am!"

"It's a mistake!"

"They're lying!"

"I'm not even supposed to be here today!"

At the reception, Nurse Margaret winced. Her headache began to feel like an expanding bruise. With practiced calm, she flipped a switch on the panel below the desk.

Overhead, and down each corridor of the ward, a series of hidden speakers crackled to life.

A painfully terrible string-and-flute muzak version of The Rolling Stones' 'Satisfaction' began to drift out. From each speaker the song played loudly, along with a handful of background static, caused by old equipment and rotting wiring. It filled the hallways, warping into something almost funereal as the cries of complaint were slowly drowned out.

Not that the inmates stopped making noises,

stopped their shouting. Now, most were happily singing along to the song.

In his cell, Trent turned his back to the door and slid down, sinking to the floor. He breathed in short gasps as he sunk into despair, lowering his head into his hands.

As he heard the music, along with the singing, he laughed mournfully. A short, breathless sound that died in his throat before it could finish.

"God..." he whispered. "...not the Stones too..."

As the storm outside began to weaken, though not enough to stop the rain, the sun had risen. It cast its glow faintly through gaps in the thick gray, pendulous clouds that hung over the institute.

Doctor Irwin Yarbrough, the institute director, sat at his desk, sweating through his shirt despite the air conditioning hissing loudly above him. A stout man in his fifties, he nervously chewed on his thumbnail as he watched the man by the window. The man wearing a governmental ID badge.

This office smelled of old coffee and bureaucracy. Yarbrough had not practiced any real medicine for years. He was now a man of forms and folders, whose only real work had been plugging holes in the sinking ship that was the institute.

At the window, dull light filtered through the blinds, casting stripes over Dr. Arthur Wrenn.

In The Mouth of Madness

A tall, narrow, unsmiling man. Wrenn was dressed in a suit, as he emotionlessly and silently read from a file in his hands.

His bony fingers turned the pages slowly, precisely, as if each page were delicate. On his government badge, clipped to his jacket, there was no photo, just a barcode and his name. Like him, the ID was clean and quite unnerving.

Yarbrough watched him with quiet desperation. He was a man in over his head, and he knew it. His lips moved once or twice, like he wanted to say something to Wrenn, to break the silence in the room, but he didn't quite dare.

Wrenn spoke, his voice quiet, as he still read.

"Admitted last night?" he asked.

Yarbrough gave a small nod. "Yeah. During the storm." There was a pause of confusion before he quickly added, "H-how did you get here so fast?"

Wrenn snapped the folder shut, making the on-edge Yarbrough flinch. "We've been monitoring admissions through police and paramedic channels," Wrenn replied, motioning to the folder. "This one fit the symptoms."

Yarbrough looked surprised, as his eyes flicked toward the folder, then back up again. "You think he's one of... them?"

Wrenn gave a thin, tight smile. "We shall see, Doctor Yarbrough. There are certainly many things about this man that are of interest."

As he moved toward the door, Yarbrough scrambled to stand up from his desk to follow. Before Wrenn could exit, the director stopped him with a hand lightly on his sleeve.

"Things must be pretty bad out there," he said, almost whispering. "To bring in you fellows. I thought you would be too busy..."

Wrenn stared back for a long, hard second. There was no reassurance in his expression, only a distant calculation as if he were measuring Yarbrough's usefulness, or capability for trouble.

Then he smiled again, barely.

"Take me to him."

The corridor in the maximum-security wing was now calm, except for the hum of fluorescent lights and the unnerving sound of string-and-flute muzak still being piped in through the old speakers, yet unlike last night, the volume was now almost a whisper. The strains of The Beatles could be heard, but a version with far too much reverb and far too little soul.

Some of the inmates murmured along, scratchy and off-key singing the words. Having been up all night screaming and yelling, they were all now half-asleep, slurring their way through the verses of 'Yellow Submarine'.

As Wrenn passed one of the speakers, he glanced up at it, then to Yarbrough.

"May I ask why?" he said, his words laced with derision.

Yarbrough smiled apologetically. His nerves were evident as if he were trying to explain away something shameful. "They... they seem to like it," he mumbled with a forced laugh. "The classics especially... Keeps them... compliant."

"Of course," Wrenn said, not really understanding nor agreeing.

As they continued, Wrenn kept his hands behind his back, eyes forward and sharp as he took in every locked door, every security camera, every scratch on the walls that paint didn't quite cover.

Yarbrough felt judged by this man's very presence. Not that he had cause to be, especially with what was going on outside these walls.

"Has he made any requests?" Wrenn asked as they turned a final corner.

"Um," Yarbrough hesitated before answering. "Just one," he said. "Nothing dangerous."

"Oh?"

"He asked for a single black crayon."

Wrenn did not reply to this. He didn't have to. His face showed a flash of disapproval before soon returning to neutral.

As they arrived at Cell Nine, Yarbrough fumbled with the keys.

Unlocking it, he pushed the door open, and both men stared in.

Yarbrough looked visibly deflated as Wrenn could not hide his amusement. A sudden crack of emotion through his granite exterior.

There were crosses everywhere.

Scrawled in thick, jagged lines, they spanned every inch of the padded cell. The walls, floor, even the ceiling. Crude, frantic, overlapped drawings. Some were simple scratches. Others were thick, waxy smears of crayon.

Even the bed was defaced. The mattress, the pillow, all covered in repeated symbols. It all appeared more desperate than holy.

Peering down, Wrenn took note of the small mound in the center of the cell, a crumpled pile of torn card wrappers. Half a dozen empty black crayon boxes.

He glanced back to Yarbrough who lingered by the doorway.

"A *single* black crayon?" he asked pointedly.

Yarbrough could only force a smile in reply.

Wrenn turned back to where John Trent was now busily drawing more crosses on a blank part of the wall. Now free from his straitjacket, he was crouched with one knee up, head bowed, as his hand worked with the last bit of whittled crayon.

Wrenn regarded him silently for a moment, before turning back to Yarbrough with a nod.

No words, just a gesture, that Yarbrough under-

In The Mouth of Madness

stood the message of immediately. He had been dismissed, and for that, he was glad. Glad to be out of the discomfort of Wrenn's glare. Without a word, the director backed away and disappeared out of the cell.

As the door clicked shut, Wrenn pulled a clean white handkerchief from his breast pocket and laid it gently on the crayon-smeared chair before sitting down, careful not to let his tailored suit touch anything more than it had to.

"John Trent?" he asked.

Trent didn't turn. His hand just kept moving, working through the last of the crayon.

One more to go.

"Hang on," Trent said, distracted.

As if concluding a ritual, he finished the final stroke on the padded wall and spun around with manic cheerfulness, tossing the nub of black crayon to the floor.

His face was also a mask of crosses. Cheeks, brow, even his eyelids stained with the same frantic pattern as the walls. He resembled a mad monk dressed for war, ready to battle in the name of a God. And that pattern continued down over his institute pajamas, covering every inch of the pale gray fabric.

"What's up?" he asked, casually sitting cross-legged on his bed. Attentive to his new visitor.

Wrenn clasped his hands together as he spoke.

"My name is Dr. Arthur Wrenn."

He paused.

"John... I'm here to try and get you out of this place, if you could help me?"

Trent's smile stayed fixed as he looked around the room like a proud homeowner.

"After all my redecorating?" he said. "Nah, you're okay. I think I'll stay right here."

Wrenn didn't flinch. "I have a guard with a pair of swollen testicles who swears you wanted out of here last night."

"That was last night." Trent shrugged with a chuckle. "Today, I think I'll take my chances in here. Had time to think, y'know? Really weigh up what's best."

"I see," Wrenn said, as he took in the room again. Slowly yet deliberately, coming to understand what was happening here. "The crosses *are* a nice touch. They'd almost *have* to keep you in here once they saw these... wouldn't they, John? Is that the point? Are you hiding?"

Trent's expression didn't change from his grin.

"You got a smoke?" he asked under his breath.

Without a word, Wrenn blindly reached into his pocket and withdrew a packet and a lighter. Taking a cigarette out, he handed it to Trent with an emotionless grace. Personally, he did not smoke. But he always carried with him two packs for occasions like these.

Trent stuck it between his lips and grinned.

Wrenn's gaze moved over the mess of crosses on

this man's face. Something about them made his eyes linger too long.

"I'm guessing it lights itself?" Trent asked, biting down on the cigarette butt.

Wrenn blinked, snapping out of his stare.

"My apologies."

He leaned forward and lit the cigarette.

Trent nodded in thanks as he took a long, slow, drawn-out drag. Holding it in for a few seconds, he then exhaled. Closing his eyes as the smoke pleasingly left his lungs.

Wrenn didn't say anything. He would let Trent initiate the next moment.

Trent saw this tactic, and shook his head, the smile now fallen to a half smirk, as he took another long drag. "You're waiting to hear about my *them*, aren't you?"

Wrenn cocked his head slightly. "Excuse me, your what?"

"My *them*." Trent opened his eyes, wide and clear as he stared. Focused. "Every paranoid schizophrenic has one, don't they? A *them*, a *they*, and *it*. The ones watching. Chasing. Whispering. Stalking and spying. The ones making me do the things I do... making me act the way I have. My Gods. My Devils. You want to hear about my *them*?"

"No, Mr. Trent, I want to know why you think you are here. I want to know your story. Your name has brought up some questions, and with what's going on, and what you have done, I wanted to speak to you. To clear up any misconceptions."

Trent didn't answer right away. He watched Wrenn, took another drag, and spoke through the smoke.

"Things are turning to shit out there, aren't they?"

Wrenn stiffened, slightly put off by the question, "Let's stay on track. Let's talk about you, shall we? The outside is quite irrelevant at present. Not your most pressing concern."

Trent smirked. "Let me ask you this," he said. "How many psychos have you seen recently, doc? How many of them had a clue?" He paused for a beat. "But *I* have a clue. But you knew that, right? You know who I am. You know my name. You want to know if it's all a coincidence?"

Wrenn reached into his pocket and pulled out a small micro-cassette recorder. Clicking it on, the tiny reel-to-reel inside began to spin with a soft whirr.

"Do you mind?" he asked.

"Do I have a say?" Trent replied playfully.

"Of *course* you do," Wrenn said, playing along, but did not find Trent's attitude amusing. "I can turn it off if you ask me to."

"I couldn't give less of a shit, record away."

"Then let's begin? Can you start by telling me about yourself?"

Trent took another drag. A long inhale. When his

In The Mouth of Madness

lungs were full, he held the smoke in as he locked eyes with Wrenn.

"I'm..." he said, finally exhaling the word through the smoke, "I *was*, I should say. I was an insurance claims investigator. Did you know that?"

Wrenn nodded.

"Worked for a firm in the city. I checked out phony claims, fraud. You know the drill. Broken backs that aren't, fires that weren't accidental, businesses that claim stock loss, when it was all just hiding out in a storage yard in Queens... that kind of thing. My job was to prove the stupidity in stupid people. People who thought that they were smarter than they actually were. It wasn't that hard to do."

He looked at the recorder. Then at Wrenn.

"But that's not why you are here. Not to hear my employment history."

"Why do *you* think I am here, Mr. Trent?" He motioned to the walls. "Are these crosses meant to ward any demon away? Are you protecting yourself or just pleading insanity?"

Trent laughed under his breath. "Don't play coy, Dr. Wrenn was it? You want to know what happened with the disappearance." His smile quickly faded. "...The *Sutter Cane* disappearance."

Wrenn said nothing. He was listening. Intently. He tried to hide his nerves, but a tremble in his lip betrayed his otherwise blank expression.

Another drag. Another exhale, and Trent continued. "Let me tell you about Hobb's End."

* * *

The Atlantic Insurance offices didn't look like much. Just a few floors in a building that was old before the moon landing and still smelled like all its past overworked employees. Fluorescent strip lighting shone across every ceiling, brightly casting a sterile glow onto the carpet, colored the shade of muddy corporate misery. One that had long since given up pretending it was ever clean.

Inside one of the small conference rooms, within its drab walls, the air was thick and uncomfortable as the air conditioning had been switched off. It was a dismal room to be in, and an even more dismal room to answer questions in.

A man sat on one side of the large table, sweating bullets into a cheap dress shirt. His name was Joseph Paul, and you could tell just by looking at him he hadn't slept in a few days. The stress was literally dripping out of him.

He was overweight, unkempt and looked prematurely defeated. Not fat like a man who enjoyed life, but fat like a man who'd been cornered by it. His jowls quivered every time he moved, as sweat fell from his skin. His tie was an outdated paisley that looked like it might've been loud in the 70s. Now, it just looked kinda sad.

Yet in his mind, he didn't see the nerves or stress being evident, he was just a bit warm and playing along with the investigation that called him in here again, to answer even more questions.

His stubby fingers fumbled with his lighter, as he brought it to the cigarette that trembled at the edge of his mouth. After a few attempts unable to flick the thing on. He smiled nervously. His hands just weren't steady enough and probably hadn't been for weeks.

Taking the lighter from Joseph's shaky grip, John Trent smiled as he flicked it alight for him, lifting it to the cigarette. His hands were calm. Sure. Rock-steady. He was not sweating and looked very well turned out. Dressed in a tailored suit that hung off him perfectly, along with perfect hair. He was clean-cut, sharp. Far from the man in Cell Nine.

"Nervous, Mr. Paul?" Trent asked, with a voice smooth and amused.

Putting the lighter on the table, he leaned back in his chair with a casual arrogance, smiling as he crossed his arms.

Sat next to him was Robinson. Balding, irritated. He didn't talk much. Just sat watching, reading the pages from an open file resting in front of him. He was the CEO of Atlantic Insurance, and liked to sit in on all the large claim meetings, and more specifically, liked to watch Trent work.

Joseph looked from Trent to Robinson, confused, nervy, and already half-defensive. "What the fuck I got to be nervous about?" he asked. His thick Jersey accent rolled out of his double chin like tar. "You told me to come down and sign some papers, so I came down to sign 'em... That's the dealio, right? I sign, I get the check." He took a stilted drag on his cigarette, as his eye twitched. "Right?"

Trent didn't answer. He just stared back. Allowing the silence to build and the pressure in the room grew. He wanted Joseph to squirm a little bit more.

On the wall behind them, a clock ticked. And that tick seemed to grow louder the longer the silence held.

Tick, tick, tick, tick, tick.

Mr. Paul's fingers twitched around the cigarette.

Tick, tick, tick, tick, tick.

Joseph could not take it anymore. He had to speak. "That's what it was supposed to be? That's what you guys said?"

"Usually, yes," Trent spoke carefully. "That's the way it goes. But I've asked you down here 'cause I just have a few final questions to ask... about the fire."

The word *fire* seemed to change the very temperature in that room, as Joseph felt his gut twist in anxiety.

He sat up straighter, looking a bit more worried. "*More* questions? I answered all your goddamn questions! Right? C'mon guys. This is cut and dry."

Trent raised a hand as a peacekeeping gesture. "Of course you have. And you've been damn cooperative.

More than most of our clients. And believe me when I say that Atlantic Insurance appreciates it."

He gestured at Robinson.

"My friend Robby here appreciates it... Don't you, Robby?"

Robinson didn't even look up from the folder. "Immensely," he said.

"See?" Trent laughed, turning back to Joseph, his smile widening. "All we need you to do is clear up a little argument Robby and I seem to be having."

"Oh?" Joseph said, feeling the tension lessening.

Trent continued. "You see, Robby here... He's the boss around here. And, well, he thinks that *you* burned down your warehouse on Northern Boulevard."

Joseph Paul exploded like a loaded spring. "What?! That's total horseshit!" he bellowed, practically leaping out of his chair. "My whole stock was in that warehouse. That was my future. My livelihood. My whole damn life."

Trent didn't flinch. He never did.

"Please calm down, Mr. Paul," he said smoothly, adjusting the cuff of his shirt like he hadn't just accused this sweaty man of arson. "Because that's exactly what I told Robby when he made such an outrageous accusation about one of our prized clients."

Joseph was unnerved by this sudden shift in tone. He started to calm, but the worry was beginning to spread behind his eyes like cracks in glass.

"Thing is, though, Robby and I have been friends

for a really long time, not to mention the man signs my checks. So, I couldn't let something like this come between us. Could I?"

He paused. Let it linger.

"*Could* I? I gotta keep my job. What he says goes, right?"

Joseph hesitated. "No... I—I guess not."

"I'm glad you understand," Trent beamed, as if they'd just settled some reasonable disagreement. "That's why I knew you wouldn't mind if I checked your story out with your wife."

That comment landed like a punch. "My wife?" Joseph asked in a whimper, the anxiety back with a sudden vengeance.

"Yeah," Trent replied casually. "See, we had these nagging little pictures of her tooling around town, wearing articles of clothing you claimed had gone up in the fire."

Robby moved an envelope from under the file he was reading. Trent took them and slid them over the table, half-spilling out the glossy photographs that were inside.

Trent waited, watching as Joseph peered down and sifted through the images. Picking them up one by one. Seeing the familiar faces. Clothes. Jewelry.

"And you know what else?" Trent added, his voice quieter now. "When I went to speak with her, your wife, she was more than eager to tell us what really happened. Especially after I showed her the pictures of Miss Rosa."

Paul stopped, as he slowly looked up from the photos.

Trent's smile turned almost predatory. "Miss Rosa," he repeated. "Who, it seems, is wearing *even more* of the articles you claimed perished in that fire on Northern Boulevard."

Another envelope was passed over by Robinson. Trent picked it up and slapped it on the table.

"Take a look," he offered.

With trepidation, Joseph picked up the envelope and opened it with shaking hands.

More photos. Another woman. Younger. More curves. Much more expensive jewelry and clothing.

"Two words of advice, my friend," Trent said casually. "If you're going to pull a scam, don't make your wife your partner."

Joseph couldn't answer. He could barely breathe. His heart was racing faster and faster.

"And if you *do* make her a partner... don't fuck around behind her back."

Paul looked immediately ruined. The photos sat scattered on the table like evidence in a courtroom. Which, in here, they were. His mouth moved slightly, but no sound came out. He had no words to defend himself.

The smoke from his cigarette drifted up toward the

Sutter Cane

strip lights above. He didn't even seem to notice embers burning down between his fingers.

Trent reached across and gently plucked the butt from his hand, stamping it out in the ashtray with a soft hiss.

Robinson, meanwhile, finally looked up from his file and closed it. His expression said everything. *Game over.*

The silence hung long, heavy and very, very final.

"People lie easily," Trent said. "Reality? That's harder to fake."

The Midtown coffee shop sat at the corner of two busy, indifferent streets, wedged between a pawn shop and a newsstand, its glass window fogged with the exhale of too many hurried lunches.

Inside, it was filled with the clatter of crockery, the noise of a dozen conversations and the hiss of food on the open grill. It smelled of burgers and eggs mixed with the relentless bubbling of coffee. Waitresses moved through the tables like traffic cops at rush hour, juggling plates and cups, as the customers ignored them.

In a booth by the window, Trent sat across from Robinson, both men nursing cups of black coffee, both feeling a quiet relief.

Trent was the picture of cool, calm efficiency. His jacket was slung neatly over the chair beside him, his tie slightly loosened. Even after a hard day, sitting in a crowded diner, he looked immaculate.

Robinson was not as cool. His shirt was wrinkled, and he looked overly exhausted.

"That was beautiful, Johnny-boy," he said, giving Trent a look of admiration laced with envy. "You got the best nose for shit I've ever seen."

Outside the window beside them, a city bus hissed to a stop. The ad plastered across its side filled the entire café window with a stark image: a jagged font screaming, *Coming Soon – In the Mouth of Madness*. Below it, the name of the infamous horror author, Sutter Cane, next to the logo of the publishing house, Arcane, in blood-red print.

The ad lingered as the bus picked up some passengers, then pulled away with a hydraulic wheeze, vanishing into the throng of the afternoon traffic.

"Best nose? Nah, we just got damn lucky this time," Trent replied, swirling his coffee lazily. "The guy's wife took a shine to me, that's all."

Robinson gave a wheezing chuckle. "You shouldn't be so modest."

"He should never have been given a policy. Men like that always try to fuck the system."

"The agents screwed up on that one. Shouldn't be to sell policies to kindergarten conmen like Joseph Paul."

"Agents?" Trent arched an eyebrow. "You mean

those guys you got on the phones? They're schmucks of the highest order."

Robinson laughed.

Trent did too, but he was not lying about his opinion. "They'd sell car insurance to blind drivers if they thought it could get them a commission. If you'd let me hire my own team to protect your company and only sell to the right people, we wouldn't have this issue. May cost you more in wages, but it would save you all this horseshit."

"I'm nearly convinced to let you do just that," Robinson replied.

Trent nodded politely with a knowing smile as he took another sip from his cup. He didn't believe a word of what Robinson said. The man was about saving money above all, not spending a cent more than needed.

"Well, I'll say it again, thank you John, you excelled as always."

"Relax, Robby," Trent replied. "That's my job. It's why you pay me as much as you do. To figure out the angles, and as you know, people are *always* looking to play an angle. God bless their crooked little hearts... They try to get away with it, but that's why you need me, to clean up the messes."

As they spoke, something was happening across the street.

A man had emerged from the shadowed lobby of the office building opposite. A pudgy, balding, short

In The Mouth of Madness

man, dressed in an ill-fitting, dull brown coat. He walked with an unsure stagger across the sidewalk, onto the street.

At a glance, he might have seemed unremarkable. A transient or someone just having a tough day. But it was the fire axe that was gripped in both hands that made people back away.

He wasn't running. But his direction was clear. He was coming for the café. Cutting a reckless path between passing cars, swinging blindly at anyone who got near.

No one took notice at first. They saw him. They saw the axe. They backed away, but didn't care too much. This was New York after all.

Inside the café, the lunch crowd didn't notice. A woman laughed too loud with a lunch date. A busboy dropped some cutlery with a clatter. Two construction workers argued about the Yankees. And Trent and Robinson sipped their coffee and spoke, without any idea of the violence threading its way toward them. Even the passing honk of car horns did nothing to bring anyone's attention to the man.

"That's good to hear," Robinson said. "Because I've got a serious mess with Arcane that I need to put you onto next. And it's a much bigger deal than some missing jewelry pay-out."

Trent raised an eyebrow. "Arcane? Should I know them?"

"Arcane Publishing," Robinson explained with a

very loud and forced sigh. "They're our biggest client and could be the thing that breaks us. I was hoping it would go away. But it seems to be sticking around."

"Never heard of 'em," Trent said with genuine surprise. He had worked for Robinson for many years and never once heard of this client.

"No reason you should have," Robinson explained. "They never file. They just take out all the policies and pay on time, and pay enough to keep the lights on... But now... Now they filed their first one and it's a doozy."

Trent found this very funny. "Doozy?"

"It could mean millions. And I need you on it as soon as possible."

Outside, the man was getting closer, and his axe had begun swinging at anyone who got close, and for the couple of people who did, they suffered a quick and brutal end. It was all happening so fast that no one had time to scream or run.

Trent raised his cup to his lips.

"What's the claim?" he asked casually, sipping.

Robinson lowered his voice.

"Sutter Cane is missing."

That name was spoken as if it held so much weight that Trent should be shocked. But he just looked blankly back at Robinson.

That's when the glass shattered.

The café window exploded inward in a storm of razor-sharp shards, as the man with the axe came crashing through the plate-glass. His entire body launched inward like a cannonball and onto the booth table where Trent and Robinson were sat.

Trent's coffee flew across his lap, burning as it fell. Robinson let out a strangled yelp, ducking just as the intruder's boots landed, tipping the Formica table and sending sugar packets and napkins scattering.

The screams around them became deafening.

People bolted for the door. Chairs fell. Trays crashed.

And still, for a breath, the man with the axe stood still in the middle of the chaos he now caused. Only approaching sirens could be heard amongst this panic.

The man turned his head slowly, scanning the café. His face twitched with eyes *too* wide. His mouth was in an almost-smile. The start of a rictus grin caused by unhinged thoughts.

And then he locked his gaze on John Trent.

Trent, frozen on the floor, looked up in fear. There was nothing he could do.

The man's leer was unblinking as he slowly leaned down. The nearer he got, the clearer Trent saw his eyes. They were subtly wrong. The proportions were slightly off. Too large for his sockets. His irises were blown and an oily blue, like liquid pools blotted on his eyeballs. They looked like something rendered in paint. Gelatinous and wet.

A strange quiet fell as the man spoke.

His voice was terrifyingly calm.

"Do you read Sutter Cane?" he asked.

Trent's mind stalled in confusion.

"Who?"

The man contorted, and the last iota of restraint snapped like a cookie. His wide eyes somehow opened even wider, and his half-grin grew into an angry snarl. He raised the axe as he let out a wild and guttural roar. The blade was about to come down, straight onto Trent, who could do nothing except try to shield himself with his arm.

And then came the gunshots.

Three of them.

Tearing their way through the man, stopping his attack.

He jerked once as the bullet ripped through his back and out his breastplate. Twice, as the second blew a hole through his throat. The third bullet slammed into his bald head, sending him forward with a shuddering cry. His grip loosened on the axe as he tumbled directly onto the table beside him, cracking it in half as it sent splinters and arterial sprays across the café.

He landed with a loud, final thud, as the axe clattered beside him.

Outside the café, two NYPD officers stood with their police-issue pistols raised, one still pointing, its barrel gently smoking. The other was on the radio, speaking frantically into his shoulder mic.

"West 45th and... and Broadway," he stuttered. "We got a situation. Multiple casualties. Suspect neutralized."

Trent slowly looked around. The screaming had stopped. Plates and chairs lay scattered. Coffee still dripped from his lap. Everyone who had not run away, now stared at the dead attacker.

The man lay sprawled across the remnants of the ruined table, his mouth slack, his eyes wide open. No longer strange or oily.

He looked... Normal. Dead.

Trent, panicked, turned to Robinson, who was sat in his chair, motionless in shock. His gaze was fixed on the blood creeping from the dead man toward his shoes.

Trent looked back at the body. Then at the shattered window. Then at Robinson.

"Who the fuck is Sutter Cane?" he said.

Chapter Two

The lights in Trent's apartment were turned low, not for ambiance but because his eyes were sore. After a long day of witnessing human stupidity that climaxed with him almost being killed, he preferred the calm, dim serenity of his home.

The place was clean, almost aggressively so. Minimalist to an extreme. In the narrow kitchen, upon the small dining table, one potted plant on its last legs rested wearily. But there was nothing on any of the surfaces. No utensils. No dishes in the sink.

In the living room, it was not much better. Couch. Television. Table. Phone. That's all. No pictures. No magazines. No books. No hi-fi.

This was the kind of home that looked staged, not lived in. To Trent, it was his Zen. His bastion of calm. He could come back here, and rest. Then go back out to work where everything was full-on all the time. He didn't need comforts. He didn't even need to cook. This was a city, and any kind of food could be bought at any hour of the day.

The television was the only light in the living room. A soft bluish flicker of grainy news footage shone over him as he watched it, sunk deep into his couch.

On-screen, it was chaos.

A shaky camera filmed a bookstore storefront. The glass had been shattered, the lighting fixture inside was hanging down to the floor. People swarmed in and around like wasps. Fists and elbows flew in this frantic mobbish melee. Some climbed over each other to get to the counter to place their order.

Outside police officers in full riot gear pushed into the mess, their nightsticks up, shields forward, as they advanced to corral this desperate crowd.

Someone screamed off-camera. It was a scream of anger and frustration as the video jolted, and the cameraman was barged to the ground, having got in the way of a desperate woman needing to get to the front.

'*This was the scene today outside several bookstores,*' the newscaster said in a sober tone. '*In New York City and all around the country, those businesses unfortunate enough to take pre-orders for horror author, Sutter Cane's, new book faced similar scenes.*'

Trent reached out and grabbed the bottle of tequila from the table in front of him and poured himself a shot into his well-used glass. The bottle clinked against the rim as he poured. His other hand was shaking. Not violently, but just enough for him to notice.

Shaking his head, he dismissed his tremble as adrenaline residue from earlier...the axe guy. The blood. Those eyes. His close call to the end.

Best not to dwell.

He put the bottle back on the table and tossed the shot back. As the tang hit his throat, he inhaled through his teeth. Cheap stuff. Not good, not terrible. Just tequila doing its job, and all he could be bothered to buy from the 7-11 before it closed.

He set the glass down, his eyes fixed on the screen.

'Cane's latest novel, In the Mouth of Madness, is already being called the biggest publishing event in recent memory,' the anchor reported evenly, as chaos continued to play out on the screen. *'Advance sales have surpassed every major release of the last ten years, and demand continues to climb, even as violence breaks out nationwide.'*

Trent felt very out of touch. People were breaking skulls over a horror novel, one written by a guy Trent had never even heard of before today. He would have chalked it down to a young person's thing, but in the video, the people rioting were of all ages.

Sutter Cane. Sounded like something a twelve-year-old would scribble on their Trapper Keeper between pentagrams. *What kind of fucking name is Sutter?* He pondered, making himself chuckle.

He reached for the remote and turned up the volume.

The feed cut to a studio setup; a polished wooden table, two talking heads facing each other. The lower third on the screen read: *Hotseat: Fiction or Faith*.

One of the commentators, a clean-cut man in his late forties with a politician's smile, spoke first.

'Today's topic on Hotseat; Sutter Cane. Harmless pop phenomenon, or deadly mad prophet of the printed page? When does fiction become religion, and are his fans as dangerous as they seem?'

The woman opposite him rolled her eyes with visible exhaustion.

'It's a book. It's just a damn book,' she sighed. *'This is more about how disenfranchisement is sweeping the nation through governmental cutbacks, forcing people to vent their anger in other areas of their life. None of this is really about a book about ghosts and ghoulies or whatever, it's about the inability to live without hardship.'*

Trent smirked. *Someone on this show still had their sanity*, he thought.

He sighed as he clicked the power off. The screen went black with a quiet *pop*, and the room went dark and silent. The light seeping in from the kitchen doing little to illuminate in here.

Are his fans really that dangerous? Trent pondered that question and recalled the man who tried to kill him today. "Yes, yes they are," he muttered to no one in particular, pouring himself another shot.

He paused for a moment, thinking about the job at hand. No matter what was happening, he still had the claim by Arcane Publishing to investigate. Normally it would excite him to search through lies to find the truth. But after today he simply felt annoyed to have to be a part of it. He didn't like being in the middle of nonsense. And this whole thing? Riots? *Murders?* But it was his job. He had no choice.

He wondered if this was all somehow manufactured. He had seen it before. Companies paying to create chaos. Sure, not to this scale, but in principle it was the same. A bit of viral marketing, drop a few cryptic posters, maybe bribe a few people to kick up a stink, create opposition to promote. Bad press is great press after all, and boom, makes millions before the first review lands. Though with this, people were dead... Arcane, if having any part of this, would have a lot to answer for beyond any insurance payout.

Paying a crowd to protest or create a stink was nothing new. Maybe all this just got out of hand. The alternative was that people were that crazy over a horror author, and to Trent, that was worrying.

Trent knocked back another shot and stood up.

Walking to the door, he picked up his leather bag, grabbed a couple of thick folders from inside, and brought them back, taking his seat on the couch again.

These were the Arcane Publishing claim files. He

hadn't read them yet, not thoroughly. He had just skimmed them after Robinson handed them over. But at the time, he could not focus. His mind was still processing the axe and the way that lunatic had asked, *do you read Sutter Cane?* like it was some kind of life-or-death question.

Trent did not fall for anything supernatural. Sure, the guy's eyes may have been... weird. No doubt about that. But weird wasn't supernatural. Weird was what happened when people did too many drugs or joined one too many conspiracy theory meetings. The world was chock full of nutcases. Always had been. Lately, maybe a few more than usual, but still, nothing mystical or otherworldly about them. Just... nuts.

He opened the top file.

Photos. Some forms. A letter from the publishing house requesting a claim payout due to their author going missing. Not kidnapped, not murdered. Just... missing. Disappeared.

He flipped the page.

Attached was a short bio of Cane. Born in New Hampshire, Yale dropout, wrote his first novel at twenty-two. Bestseller list by twenty-five. Now his books were translated into eighteen languages and were apparently outselling Stephen King by over ten times, despite having only six novels released.

Cane's picture was stapled to the corner of the form. A grainy author headshot, mid-forties, rough features, wireframe glasses, a curly mop of hair. He looked like every smug writer Trent had ever seen before.

Nothing special. A faux intellectual who merely had a better grasp of English than his readers.

Still... the fans. The way they were behaving. It didn't sit quite right. Not because Trent thought there was anything *real* to the hysteria. Just that it wasn't logical. People didn't riot over horror books, especially over a *pre-order*. The book wasn't even out yet!

If it all was a stunt, it was the dumbest yet the most genius campaign ever. And no doubt, no matter what he would discover during the investigation, nothing would stop the book becoming a best seller.

Still nothing about any of this felt... real. Not in the way it apparently did to everyone else. The bookstore riots? Cult-like hysteria. The axe guy? Mentally ill. Or dosed. Probably both. Sutter Cane? A delusional writer who finally got lost in his own bullshit. Maybe he'd pulled a disappearing act to boost sales. Maybe he was already in Aruba, drinking Mai Tais and laughing at everyone.

Whatever it was, Trent would find the answer. That's what he did.

He closed the top file. He couldn't be bothered reading any more.

Whatever it was, it *wasn't* a mystery.

It was a job. Either it was a lie or was the truth. If a lie, it would be business as usual. If the truth... Then he may not have a job anymore, if his company had to pay out what was asked.

So, tomorrow, he'd begin.

He looked at his watch. 2:48 a.m.

Great, he thought. *Too late to get a good sleep.*

* * *

The illustration was beyond vivid.

It wasn't just detailed but drawn to look almost photo-realistic, which made it all the more disturbing. It was as if it had been shot through a camera lens aimed at the bowels of a nightmare.

In it, a circle of children stood in the middle of a cemetery, caught in mid-transformation. They were each changing. Changing into something grotesque. Their skin bubbled and writhed as their mouths stretched open in silent agony. From every orifice over them, tentacles emerged like worms. Breaking through broken teeth and from the middle of their eyeballs. Bloody and very wrong, each tentacle reached skyward. Their small bodies were contorting into something else. No, not contorting so much as *becoming*.

In the middle of them was something else. A hulking shape, its edges blurred as if the artist couldn't quite commit to rendering it in ink. A vague, mountainous wrongness made of fangs, claws and even more

In The Mouth of Madness

tentacles, all looming out of the middle of the monstrous circle. In the distance was an old, black church, complete with old onion-domes. In all a terrifyingly strange piece of art.

The title scrawled beneath the image read, *The Lesson by Sutter Cane.*

Trent stared at it. His brow furrowed as he tried to grasp why this even existed. Who it was for. He understood that it was cover art. But why *that*? Who would want to see *that*?

He didn't know how long he'd been looking at it, hung in a frame on the wall of the managerial offices at Arcane Publishing, but the receptionist had called him twice already, and he had not heard.

"Mr. Trent? Hello?" she asked again.

The voice came, expertly hiding its contempt behind a façade of civility.

Trent turned and blinked, as if waking up.

"Mr. Harglow will see you now," the receptionist said, moving back to the book she was reading. She was sat behind a tall desk, cold and metallic. She looked striking in that fashion-magazine way: flawless skin, eyes sharp as razors that sat behind designer glasses. A walking mannequin with perfect posture and a bloodless sort of beauty.

Trent glanced once more at the picture, then let it go.

The wall was lined with other such framed illustrations. All disturbing works of photo-realistic art. All signed by the artist of the same name. Sutter Cane.

He created these too?

In each of them, images of mutated people, mutated architecture, and a same crooked, onion-domed, black church. Each was cover art for his books.

Walking up to the reception, Trent could not help but see an eight-foot-tall cardboard standee. It was for Cane's previous release, *The Hobb's End Horror*. More monstrous people, that church, a stormy sky, a clawed monster. *Urgh*... Trent had only just seen these, but already he was tired of them. It was all so childish to him.

He gestured lazily toward it.

"You get tired of looking at this crap?"

The receptionist was too busy reading to pay him any attention.

He noticed that it was a Sutter Cane book in her hands. *Of course it was.*

She slowly looked up from the pages, having just finished the paragraph, her eyes meeting Trent's with all the warmth of a mortician.

"Guess not," he mumbled.

She turned her eyes back to the text, disinterested.

A trickle of red suddenly leaked from one of her nostrils. She dabbed at it absently with a Kleenex, already half-stained with blood and buried herself back in the story.

Trent had not noticed any of it. He was already

pushing through the next door, lost in confusion as to what it was that Sutter Cane had over everyone. What made them so damn odd.

People ask the wrong questions.

They wonder about the subjects I write. What my stories mean. What the tales could do to people. As if meaning was the point.

It is not.

The story is just the icing. The sweetness to swallow the pill.

The real work happens underneath.

You ever see someone read one of my books? Really read one? They don't flip through it. They sink. Their eyes stop blinking. Their lips start moving. Like they're repeating it back to themselves. Like they're learning the words for something they have to rehearse.

But don't hold it against anyone for thinking that the books are merely tales. They will come around.

The office was grand in the way that only old money could buy, dark oak furniture, shelves of unread hardcovers, brass... well, everything. And the man sat behind the desk could have been carved from that very same wood. With grey hair, precise posture, a face rich with lines making his stern expression, he was a stately, humorless man in his late sixties. The CEO of Arcane Publishing, the man making the insurance claim, Jackson Harglow.

"Mr. Trent," he said, rising only slightly from his chair. "Please, sit down."

Trent did.

"I'm Jackson Harglow," he said. "Are you familiar with Arcane?"

"You're insured by the company I work for," Trent said matter-of-factly. "Beyond that, not really. Sorry."

A second voice joined the room from the other side. Female. Sharp. Playfully sarcastic.

"Do you read much?" she asked.

Trent turned toward the voice.

She stood quietly, confidently. Late twenties, red hair tied back, and a pair of thin glasses. Her gaze was quite cutting, half-amused, half-dismissive, and carried a lot of power. The kind of woman who was not only the smartest person in the room but was tired of having to prove it.

"I read one once," Trent shot back. "Didn't think much of it. Not really needed in what I do."

She smiled as she moved and stood next to Harglow. Not with a full smile, but enough of one to make Trent's heart jump slightly in his chest.

"Allow me to introduce Linda Styles," Harglow said. "One of our top editors. She has worked exclusively with our most successful author. Perhaps you've heard of him... Sutter Cane?"

Trent played dumb. He was good at that. It gave people just enough rope to hang themselves. Not that he knew much of the man he'd only heard of 24 hours ago, and nothing beyond the vague biography page he glossed over.

"That horror crap, right? Monsters and kids' stuff?"

Styles didn't flinch, but her eyes slightly narrowed. "Sutter Cane happens to be the most widely read author of this century," she said. "You can forget Stephen King; Cane outsells them all."

"With Sutter Cane," Harglow added, "we've found that people seem to be consistently drawn to the twisted, and freakish. And with that comes money. And with money comes a lot of problems."

Trent was not impressed by any of this. "I live in New York. I see that kinda stuff every day. Doesn't mean I wanna read about that crap."

Harglow smiled, ignoring the veiled insult of his client. "Which is why you are best suited for this, Mr. Trent. Better to have an unbeliever."

Trent liked both Harglow and Styles immediately. Not because they were nice, or accommodating, but because he could already sense a challenge. Something in the way they talked that smacked of bluster. And beneath that bluster was a lie wrapping its fist around the truth.

Harglow continued. "I've asked Linda here

because she has particular relevance to this... situation."

"Which is what, exactly?" Trent asked.

Harglow clasped his hands together tightly as he rested them on the desk. As he spoke, there was a weight to the words, like they were difficult to say.

"Sutter Cane... Sutter Cane vanished," Harglow said. "Vanished completely. Without a trace. Approximately two months ago."

Trent looked at every shift Harglow made in his seat and every stutter of his words. He may have appeared genuine, but Trent was looking beyond that. He was analyzing everything about how the words were being said.

Trent raised an eyebrow. "And the Police?"

"Of course, we contacted them," Styles interjected. "But they've turned up nothing."

That was the one lie most fakers made without backing up. Liars always pretended to have done all they could. But with all cases, Trent would check each claim out. He would look for filed police reports, as 90% of the time, no matter how big the claim, how expert the liar, claiming police involvement was usually the first provable mistake people would make. Sensing lying to the cops was harder than lying to an insurance company. *How wrong they were.*

"We have a copy of our police filings here," Harglow said as he slid a couple of sheets of paper across the desk to Trent, taking him somewhat by surprise. "Feel free to validate these."

Nice play, Trent thought.

"Who was the last to hear from Cane?" he asked.

"His agent," Harglow replied. "Cane supposedly sent him a portion of the new manuscript not more than two weeks ago... Plain brown wrapper, no return address."

"What'd the agent have to say?"

There was a pause, followed by an exchanged look between Harglow and Styles.

"What is it?" Trent said, not appreciating the sudden coyness.

Styles was the one who eventually answered.

"You heard what he had to say," she said. "You were there."

Trent frowned. "Excuse me?"

"In Midtown," Harglow added. "Apparently you were there when the poor man lost it. I believe you saw him shot by the police."

Trent gasped quietly, letting the weight of the realization and coincidence sink in. "You mean that lunatic with the axe? That was Cane's *agent*?"

"Hard to believe, isn't it?"

Trent could not contain his amusement. "Jesus. You'd think a guy who outsells Stephen King could find better representation."

No one else was laughing, and that's the way Trent liked it. Everything he said and did was intentional.

Practiced. With a point. And now both Harglow and Styles thought that he was a fool and were caught off guard. Exactly what he needed.

Trent let this uncomfortable silence stretch, then broke it.

"So, what's the theory? He reads the latest chapter and decides to go on a midday murder spree?"

"This is no joke Mr. Trent," Styles said, still unamused. "Cane's books have been known to have an effect on his readers. We have spent a significant amount of money setting up customer helplines for that very thing."

"How're *you* holding up, then?" Trent asked, not falling for the pitch she was selling. "Seeing as you edit his stuff?"

Styles offered the faintest grin. "I'm just fine."

"Linda's one of the few editors brave enough to take on editing Cane's work," Harglow added. "He is quite demanding."

"What happened to the other editors?"

"Nausea. Migraines. Hallucinations. One had a seizure. Another... a heart attack that they unfortunately did not recover from... and nosebleeds. Lots of nosebleeds."

Trent snorted, not buying a word of it. "Sounds like a hell of a PR campaign." He didn't let Harglow or Styles get a word in. "And you think Cane's agent took one look at the latest masterpiece of monsters and goblins and went axe-happy in broad daylight? What a way to sell a new book. The publicity will be off the charts."

"This isn't a hoax, Mr. Trent," Harglow said, his voice suddenly sterner than his expression. "You were there. You saw it. Surely you believed your own eyes. Does that man's death look like a hoax?"

Trent hesitated. "Point taken. But it all still seems so convenient, you see that, right?"

"We have no desire to publicize Cane's connection to this... incident," Harglow said. "We're trying to *avoid* any negative connotations. We simply want Cane back. We want the book finished. As quietly as possible. We have millions of pre-orders in, and no book to give them. Aside from the sample chapters Styles has, and whatever the agent was sent we are still to get our hands on."

"Sutter Cane's franchise makes up eighty percent of Arcane's income," Styles added. "We've already delayed the release by a month already. But his fans... they're getting restless."

"Rioting-in-a-bookstore restless." Trent said.

"Or worse," Styles replied.

Harglow cut in. "We need to know if Sutter Cane is alive, or dead. Obviously, there's a great deal of money at stake. We're already in the middle of a very expensive campaign."

"Well, if I'm going to find your golden goose," Trent said. "I'll need to see his papers. Addresses. Financials."

"You can see what little we have, but most you will not be able to." Harglow said flatly. "Cane's agent handled all the legal affairs. A total buffer. We don't even know where Cane lived. We have his signing contract, the book contracts, but all through the agent. Nothing else."

Trent raised an eyebrow. *Surely that was a lie.* "You're telling me your biggest cash cow is basically a ghost, and not once did you get any way to contact him?"

Styles' expression turned to one that Trent had not seen in any of his claim meetings. Actual concern. Either she was not in on whatever was happening, or she was putting on an Academy Award worthy performance.

"All we know is that in the months before he disappeared, his work became... unhinged... Bent. His agent told us that when he spoke to Cane, that he started to believe the stories were real. That his *characters* were real. That the places he wrote about were more than fiction."

"This is more about the book than the man, if I'm honest Mr. Trent," Harglow added, "We need the chapters. That's all. If Cane wants to remain wherever he is, that is not our concern. We just need our property."

Trent stared at them. If this was a ruse, both people were playing an expert hand.

"Read his work, Mr. Trent," Harglow said. "It may

help you get to know about him more."

Styles smiled. A smile that held no comfort. "Or it might do more than that."

"Is that a threat, Ms. Styles?" Trent asked.

"Consider it a challenge. To see if you like, what did you say? The monsters and goblins?"

Trent wandered through the bookstore's horror section with the same level of enthusiasm someone might have while shopping for drain cleaner. His expression said it all: he felt ridiculous, and very bored by everything.

Staring at the glut of mass-market paperbacks, their garish and gory covers, he felt like some kind of elaborate joke was being played but was unsure at who the punchline was meant to humiliate. Him or the people that read this stuff.

The shelves were awash with King, Herbert, Matheson, but one author's books outnumbered all of them together... Sutter Cane.

Trent had not appreciated how big this author was. In fact, stood here. He felt a bit dumb that he had not even heard of him.

And it was not just the books. Posters hung overhead. Standee displays stood at the end of most shelves. Promotional cards on the countertops. The name of Cane's missing manuscript was everywhere

here. The same stylized font stared back at him: *In The Mouth of Madness – Coming Soon*.

He reached out, plucked one of Cane's books from the shelf, then another. Then all six. *The Thing in the Basement. The Breathing Tunnel. The Feeding. The Haunter Out of Time. The Whisperer of the Dark. The Hobb's End Horror*. He felt absurd, and a bit embarrassed as the titles stared back at him.

"I can see," a voice said, small, young, and far too close to Trent.

Turning, he saw a boy looking up at him, no more than eight years old. Pale. Feverish. His skin looked almost waxy. His blue eyes stared at Trent as he clutched a copy of *The Hobb's End Horror* as if it were his favorite teddy bear. The oversized glasses he wore had been snapped on the bridge and been fixed with Scotch tape. His nose ran steadily and unbothered over his lip. A scab on his chin gleamed red and raw. He picked at it as he spoke.

"I can see," he said again.

"Excuse me?" Trent said, genuinely unsettled. "See what?"

"*He* sees you."

A chill crept down Trent's back, subtle but there. He forced a smile, glancing around for the kid's parents, but he could see no one else.

"Your parents let you read this stuff?" he asked, attempting to soften the edge in whatever the hell was happening.

The kid blinked slowly and suddenly looked annoyed. He looked at Trent as if he were an idiot. "*Everyone* reads Sutter Cane."

Trent shrugged and turned away. The boy stood watching him as he made a beeline for the cash register, bought the books and left the store. Even as Trent walked by the window and looked in, the boy was still standing in the same place, still staring at him.

Chapter Three

The subway platform was a gray slab of cement and fluorescent lights. DeKalb Avenue station had never looked that welcoming, but tonight it felt especially sour. Trent paced with the plastic bookstore bag hanging from his wrist. Inside were the six Sutter Cane books he felt he had no choice but to buy. Reluctant research that was now just an annoying weight.

A train rumbled down an adjacent platform. As Trent's eyes followed its journey through the station, his eyes caught on a series of posters pasted onto one of the tiled walls.

It was for *The Hobb's End Horror*. Sutter Cane seemed to be following him around like a bad smell. The book had been released eleven months ago but was still being advertised as if it were brand new. And now Trent was seeing it everywhere. He had only glimpsed into Cane's world for a day, but he was already tired of seeing his stupid name and stupid art everywhere he went.

But as he peered at the three identical posters pasted side by side. Something about them caught his eye. Though he did not know what.

The upper corner of one of the posters had peeled away from the wall. Ever so slightly. The tiniest fold that curled out. That wasn't weird at all. Not for a sloppily pasted up poster. Not in the subway. But now... Trent felt... He did not know *what* he felt.

He stepped closer to the poster.

His fingers reached out to the curled corner, pinching at it.

He pulled gently, slowly revealing a darker layer beneath. Another poster. Another advert. Shiny. Black.

Before he could examine it further, his train pulled up to the platform behind him, ripping his attention away from the wall, blasting wind and screaming toward him. He let go of the paper corner, and it curled back against the wall, covering whatever lurked beneath.

Trent felt a pang of disgust. The subway car was a festering sardine tin as it always was. Rush hour had ended, but New York never truly emptied. Especially not down in the subway. He stood wedged between an incredibly large woman dressed in a floral muumuu, and a pimple-covered teenage boy, who blasted tinny, headache-inducing synth from the headphones of his brick-sized Walkman.

The whole car stank of rancid sweat and piss and was a testament to the despair of everyone forced to travel on it. Trent hated, but always had to endure it.

He didn't try to find a handrail. He would not hold onto one of those even if a gun was held to his head. So, he stood with his legs slightly apart, bracing his movement. He also had to angle his head to breathe through his mouth, and not smell the people pressing on him, but it didn't help.

His fingers tightened around the plastic bag of books. Books he would have rather not spent eighty bucks on.

He avoided any eye contact as best he could, until, unintentionally, he saw someone. On the far corner of the car, an obviously drunk, homeless man sat hunched in his seat, crusted and browning as if he'd been left in a filthy gutter too long, with a long streak of urine damping his muck-caked trousers. But it wasn't the dirt or piss that made Trent's stomach shift, it was the man's stare.

He was looking straight back at Trent with a focused, intent azure-eyed glare.

Trent tried to look away. But as he did, something tickled at his mind. Some awful curiosity that made him look back...

... and the man hadn't stopped.

But now, in addition to the stare, *his lips were moving*. Slowly. Silently.

Repeating words.

Trent could not help as he tried to read his lips. Through the man's broken teeth and overgrown beard, the words were clear: *I can see.*

The man then shut his eyes.

And just like that, in an instant, the dirty man was asleep. With mouth falling open. Passed out like he'd never been anything else.

As if on cue, the train shuddered to a sudden halt as the wheels screeched and whined against the rails beneath them. Everyone in the carriage, including Trent, was thrown even harder together, slamming into each other as the car emergency stopped.

A chorus of angry groans and startled curses erupted around him. One voice barked about being late, another cursed the city, and as they did, the muffled voice of the driver could be heard from the speakers lining the car.

'*Uhhh, attention passengers,*' he said in a broad New York accent. '*Sorry for this delay. We should be movin' along shortly.*'

As soon as he stopped talking, the lights snapped off.

The subway car was immediately plunged into black, and people's complaints rose from mumbles to shouted annoyance.

"Get off my foot, you fat bitch!"

"Hey, watch the umbrella!"

"What the fuck is going on?"

"—*and turn that fuckin' music down!*" another bellowed, as the pimple-faced teenager's Walkman continued to blare loudly through his headphones.

An hour later, Trent emerged from the Bay Ridge subway exit. He looked drained. Not just of energy, but patience and calm. The train's lights eventually turned back on, and they resumed their journey, with now much irate and volatile passengers.

The weather above started to match Trent's gloom as rain started to drizzle down. Like the rest of the day, this was not anger-inducing, but it was even worse... it was just annoying. The bookstore. The broken-down subway. The whole business with Arcane... it all annoyed Trent greatly.

The Sutter Cane disappearance had started to grate. Not just because he thought that Harlow or Styles were lying, but because they were just so damn good at it, which made his investigation that much more difficult. Sure, he loved a challenge, but now with the agent dead and no one else to question, he felt like the whole thing was a tangled ball of yarn that he could not find an end to pull at.

With the bag of books still in hand, he grabbed a cigarette from the pack in his jacket pocket, lit it, then crossed the street to a nearby alleyway. A shortcut he'd taken almost every night.

Tonight was different. As he approached it, he could hear a strange sound coming from the shadows.

Thump, thump, thump.

Heavy and uneven.

He paused for a moment.

Thump, thump, thump.

Edging forward, his eyes began to adjust to the darkness within, to the low light that shone from a back door of the nearby tenement.

He could see where the sound was coming from, and as he got closer, he started to be able to see more and more details.

It was a uniformed police officer, towering over a scrawny boy slumped against a brick wall. The kid couldn't have been more than mid-teens, unconscious, limbs limp. Without hesitation, the cop raised his nightstick and brought it crashing down on the boy's already shattered arm, once, twice, again... each blow heavier than the last.

Thump, thump, thump.

Beside them, a spray can rolled slowly through a shallow puddle. Above, still wet and dripping red down the alley wall, fresh graffiti read: *I CAN SEE.*

Sensing someone watching him, the cop quickly paused his assault. Turning, before Trent could even think of turning away, their eyes locked on each other.

"You want some too, buddy?" the cop growled, waving the nightstick threateningly.

Trent didn't answer. He couldn't. He just turned and walked away as fast as he could.

None of this was his business.

He hurried out of the alley, electing to walk the long way home. And behind him, the brutal beating soon resumed. The sound carrying out toward him: *Thump, thump, thump.*

The lights were off in Trent's apartment, all except for the old, brass reading lamp perched beside the couch. Its pale circle of light cast onto the open book in Trent's hands, what the front cover billed as 'The Third Sutter Cane Nightmare... *The Feeding.*'

He didn't notice the silence around him. He didn't notice the dark. He was buried in the words. Eyes scanning line after line. He was not caught up in the story at all. In fact, he was reluctantly forcing himself to finish each line... But it was something about the writing. Its rhythm. It had an almost grotesque poetry in its overtly purple prose. One that frankly disgusted him. But still, he kept turning the pages. That was the worst part of it. He was not enjoying it, but he was not putting it down.

His face grimaced with revulsion at a particularly nasty passage. A woman giving birth to a sludgy beast.

Sutter Cane

Teeth first. It was vile. And brutal. And brilliant. And vile.

His fingers gripped tighter around the book's spine. He hated this. Hated how the book made him feel as if he were *breathing someone else's air*. Hated how—

—the phone rang loudly, making him jolt. Almost louder than it was possible to sound. A shrill stab of noise that punctured the silence and Trent's concentration like a splinter through his eardrums.

He sat for a moment, teeth still clenched from the surprise. Embarrassed at his sudden fear of the noise. A phone he had heard a million times. He was embarrassed that a book, *a damn book*, had wound him up that tight. A book about sludgy baby monsters.

He reached up and pinched the bridge of his nose, squeezing hard, trying to push the tension out through his skull.

The phone, meanwhile, continued to ring. Each chime screaming at him.

The subway car was full... yet again, as always.

Packed shoulder to shoulder with people carrying all the stink and noise of the city with them. Each squished tightly against each other behind the clacking doors.

The overhead lights had the same jaundiced glow, shining the same bleakness across the worn-out passengers.

Trent was there too. Only now, he was not standing up between anyone.

He was sitting, low and hunched on one of the end seats. He did not wear a suit as normal, instead, he wore a homeless wino's coat now. Stained and shapeless, with an abhorrent stench of waste coming off it.

The plastic bag full of Sutter Cane books sat on his lap.

But he wasn't the only one looking at it.

All around the car, passengers were staring back. Not directly at him, but also at the bag. At the books he carried.

Someone coughed.

Another scratched at their scalp until blood showed.

The boy with the broken glasses from the bookstore was at the far end, unmoving, his hollow eyes fixed on the bag.

As before, the subway train suddenly grounded to a halt. Whining as the wheels gripped the rails beneath them.

People were flung onto one another as the whole car lurched.

Over the sounds of people complaining, the driver could be heard from speakers.

'*Uhhh, attention passengers,*' he said in a broad New York accent. '*Sorry for this delay. We should be movin' along shortly.*'

Then, also as before, the lights snapped off.

Sutter Cane

The whole train was immediately plunged into darkness.

"Get off my foot, you fat bitch!"

"Hey, watch the umbrella!"

"What the fuck is going on?"

Trent found himself opening the door to the subway and walking out onto the tunnel's tracks.

Behind him, the passengers were still moaning at the sudden stoppage.

"*—and turn that fuckin' music down!*" one of them bellowed to the pimple-faced teenager.

He did not know why, but dressed in the wino's clothes, carrying his bag of books, Trent walked on. His footsteps echoed around him with each uncertain step. The only light here within the train behind him, casting long shadows along the dank tunnel.

As he walked further from the train, from the shouting complaints of the passengers, another sound ahead caught his attention.

Thump, thump, thump.

The same familiar uneven beats he heard before. The same sound of meaty impacts.

He carried on walking, around the snaking corner of the tunnels.

And there it was.

The cop.

Thump, thump, thump.

Still pounding his nightstick mercilessly down on

the same kid. Whose body was a mangled pile of twitching limbs and bloodied clothing. The words *I CAN SEE* had been spray painted in big, black letters along the tunnel wall behind him.

The cop didn't stop as Trent got closer.

Thump, thump, thump.

His beats soon started to slow, until finally he stopped, straightened, and calmly turned.

What looked back at Trent was not a man.

The thing that faced him wore the clothing of a cop, but the thing's proportions were all wrong. His arms were too long, as if they had been stretched and swollen. Fingers like branches, knuckles blackened. This thing's skin was bloated, grey, pallid, and cracked like something dredged from the bottom of the ocean. Its mouth was too large and wide, its eyes, as it now stared directly at him, glowed a pale blue in the dark, oily and bulbous.

"You want some too, buddy?" it asked, its voice distorted and grinding, as if through a broken speaker at full volume.

Trent didn't answer.

He just ran as fast as he could, back down the tracks, down the tunnel, back toward the subway car, desperate to escape.

But as he got close, and the train came into view, the doors had opened, and the passengers were now walking out.

One after another.

Calm.

In procession.

No talking. No shouting. No complaining. No humanity.

Each clutched in their hands, an axe.

This mob were being led by someone.

The man from the café.

Cane's agent. Looking just as he did before.

His shirt was still soaked with his own dried blood. The exit wound in the center of his face had crusted black and red, his jaw hung slack and drooled thick, ropy saliva mixed with dark bloody clots. His head twitched to the side with every step, like hanging from a damaged wire. But yet, he still smiled. Wide and proud.

"It's a good read," he slurred through his torn mouth, eyeing Trent as he came to a stop. "It's a goooood reeeeeaad.".

The other passengers started to circle him, and he didn't seem to mind. It made him smile even more gleefully. More perversely.

He didn't run. Didn't beg. He stood in the middle, tongue wetting his lips in anticipation and did not break eye contact with Trent.

And then the axes came down.

Not one of the passengers hesitated.

The first blow landed in the middle of the agent's

collarbone, splitting skin, bursting through bone. The second cleaved into the back of his knee, folding him over onto the ground until Trent could not see him anymore. He only saw his executioners, hacking over and over with their axes.

He may not have seen any more, but he heard it.

He could hear the wet crunch of bone reverberating around the tunnel's walls.

He could hear the joyous screams of the agent as he was being murdered. Still calling out to Trent, even as he was being ripped apart.

"A GOOD READ! A GOOD READ! ARRGGGGH!"

When his noises stopped, every head turned, straight toward Trent.

No one said a word.

The fat woman in the muumuu moved to the front now. Her dress soaked in gore, chunks of flesh clinging to the floral print. Her eyes were bulging. The grin she wore was almost identical to the one they'd just hacked off their victim.

She took a step forward.

"He *sees* you," she said. And they all began to step closer.

Trent stumbled, breath escaping from his lungs in a panic, as he spun around to escape...

...running straight into the arms of the monstrous cop.

The thing opened its enlarged mouth, as it raised its crimson-dripping nightstick. Ready to bring it down ...

...Trent woke with a choking gasp.

Soaked in sweat, his heart slammed in his chest as if it were trying to break out.

He sat forward on the couch frantically, running both hands through his sweaty, matted hair, accidentally knocking the stack of Cane books over on the table as he did. Sending them scattering in front of him.

"Fuck," he muttered, gathering his bearings. Shutting out the fear that had dragged him back to reality. "Freaky fucking shit."

Linda Styles' apartment sat at the edge of the Upper East Side, up two flights of cracked concrete stairs in a building that had seen better decades. Even so, it was a wealthy neighborhood.

As Trent walked through the entrance, he wondered how much a book editor earned that would mean she could afford to live here. From the lobby, up the stairs to the hallway outside her door, it smelled like old wood. Not damp but polished. Sure, it was an elderly structure, but it was cared for, despite its wrinkles.

Inside, the apartment was dark.

Then came the knocking.

Loud. Fast. Persistent, with a very obnoxious rhythm.

Styles, riled from a deep sleep, grabbed her bathrobe and threw it on as she blearily padded up the hallway, stubbing her toe hard against the umbrella stand on her way.

"*Damnit*," she hissed, stumbling.

The knocking continuing.

"Alright!" she called out, getting to the door.

The light from the hallway crept in under the crack of the door as she switched on her own. She checked her watch; it was almost midnight. Not looking impressed, she slipped the chain across, and opened the door, cracking it just enough to see who was disturbing her at this time.

Trent stood on the other side. Wearing a smile that was either disarming or smug, she could not tell. In his hand was a white paper bag, soaked through with grease.

"I brought Chinese," he said, as if it were a peace offering... as if they knew each other more than the one meeting they had earlier.

She stared in disbelief.

"How'd you get my address?" she asked, not bothering to hide her irritation.

"Company roster," he said casually.

"And this couldn't wait until tomorrow?"

"You said it was important. And I had some urgent things I needed to discuss."

"Urgent? You've been on the case for two days. I'll be in the office in nine hours. What could you have possibly found that made you traipse all the way here, uninvited, waking me up?"

"Can I come in? Just for a few minutes."

In her kitchen, Styles sat at the edge of the table, chopsticks reluctantly poking at a box of steamed vegetables with zero enthusiasm.

"So, what is it?" she asked.

Trent grabbed one of the bottles of beer he had brought, twisted the cap off and took a sip.

"The tingling's happened." He grinned.

"The what?"

He nodded, like it explained everything. "It's this buzz I get, just behind the eyes, when things start to click. Like a little itch in my head. That's how I know I'm close. And if you want this wrapped up quickly, and that eighty percent of your company's revenue remaining intact..."

She raised an eyebrow, lifting a limp piece of broccoli. "Tingling? You sure it's not the MSG in this shit?"

"Positive. That's only responsible for my lockjaw," he said, deadpan.

She smirked. Not encouragement. Not forgiveness. Just deadpan amusement.

For a second, something hung there, something unspoken, a reluctant spark between them neither had invited nor welcomed. She hated it. The man was rude. Arrogant. And he hated it too. This woman was cold. Lying.

"I've been skimming Cane's stuff," Trent said. "A cursory read of them, and already I've seen tells."

Styles rolled her eyes. "Tells?"

"Maybe you missed them while editing them. Or maybe you saw it and didn't care. But there's a distinct pattern that feeds into what's happening."

She arched an eyebrow.

"They all talk about another race. Something older. Stronger."

"Yeah, that's the story arc to all his books. The world Cane built has Lovecraftian DNA. Ancient gods lived in this reality, lost their foothold, and are trying to come back. Cane just gave it all a pulpy twist. It's nothing new, Cane just did it damn *well*."

"Yeah," he said, opening a notebook he pulled from his pocket. "But that's all a lot of people will read. Different stories, different characters, with those monsters trying to come back to reality... but there are connective tissues beneath that. Like different characters in the books have the same beats. Always some guy in them who leaves or wants to walk away from his life. Disappear totally. Sometimes he's a painter, sometimes a writer, sometimes just some guy in a dead-end job, it doesn't matter. Every book has one that leaves or talks about leaving. They check out. And it always leads back to Hobb's End. Always."

She frowned. "So what? That's pulp. That's horror. Cane has motifs. Repetition in horror is key."

"No, Styles, motifs are *themes*. This is a structure. Recurrence. Like he's telling the same story over and over, just dressing it up a bit differently each time. And each time, he gets closer to saying something outright. By *Hobb's End Horror*, he's not even pretending or making up stuff. As the narrator, he literally says he's moving to Hobb's End. Not visiting. Moving to. He wrote himself into the fucking story. He started in the first book as that guy who leaves the city to come see his family. Comes to Hobb's End. Then after that, Cane starts actually writing in the book as himself. And that last one basically had him coming in and changing the story that was being told. Influencing it."

She folded her arms. "It's called meta-fiction. It's a device. Cane always asserts himself as the narrator. Poses a deeper meaning to his stories. Allows him to affect the reader."

"Or," Trent countered, "it's him telling us. Telegraphing his plays. Like he planned the whole disappearing act, and this is the smoke he left behind.

The characters in the books were him wanting to get out. And he just said it. He was leaving to go there."

Styles snorted. "You think he planned this over his whole career?"

"No? Yes?... subconsciously maybe? It's like he tried a story, released it, then rewrote it, just changing the plot part." Trent flipped through his notebook. "The town shows up in every book. Fine. Writers reuse settings. But it's not just that. It's how the *details* line up."

"They're supposed to line up," Styles said, "It's world-building."

"No," he said, tapping a note. "You're not hearing me. The *first* time Hobb's End is mentioned, it's a throwaway. One line. And all it had is that diner off a highway, right? The town is Eagle Heights. In the next book, it's called Hobb's End, and it's got a post office. A church. A school. Next book he put a street map in there. It's bigger. Growing. It's not just reused. It's *added to*, book by book. Same layout. Same street names. Even the same minor characters. Each one is expanded. You realize what that means?"

Styles didn't.

"It means these weren't different stories. They were just rewrites. Six books, each telling a different story, but in each one he was just filling in blanks. It's like Cane wasn't writing the developing story, he was telling the story of the location. Like he was slowly sketching out the borders of something real and just throwing a story on top of it. Something he couldn't do straight away."

She looked very skeptical. "You need some sleep. This is dumb."

"How do you explain Elijah Kirby?" He scans from the page. "This character here. In one book runs at the butcher shop. Next, he is a postal worker. Next, he is on the town council. No speaking lines. Shows up in *five* different books. Same name. Same face. No fanfare. Just... there. Mentioned as a name. But *each* time, he does something different, until the last one where he mentions that Hobb's End has a laundromat, something he never did before. And who is the manager of that laundromat? And apparently had been for twenty years? Contradicting the last books? Elijah fucking Kirby."

"This is all a bit loose of a theory?"

"Cane never references him as a real character. Not once. No Easter eggs, no self-awareness. Not even a wink. He's *just there*. Over and over. But he's the guy who is in the new places that Cane writes about. Like Cane didn't want him in his books, but he was in all the new places he was writing anyway. And you say Cane is not a bad writer, so what is it? Is Elijah Kirby intentional or bad writing?"

"This is what your tingling tells you? That each book is the same story, Cane lives in Hobb's End, and he writes characters he doesn't want to write?" She laughed. "Let me tell you right now Hobb's End isn't real. It's a *fiction*. Just like Elijah Kirby. Someone Cane made up and wrote a name to add flavor to the stories. He is not important. It's just to throw you off. Contradict to disrupt. It's not dumb, its genius actually. Makes the reader doubt their memory. And as for the stories being rewrites of each other? That's the stupidest thing I've heard in a while."

"No, you misunderstand me. This... it's all guesswork... What my tingling tells *me*," he said, lowering his voice, "is that this stinks of Cane intending to do this. I don't know why. But I think his writing was somehow him exorcising his own demons. And Hobb's End, whichever real town he based that on. He's *there*."

She was already shaking her head.

"So, I need you to just cut to it," he said. "Tell me straight. If you know, tell me why now. And I promise no one will find out you've tipped me... I get it, it's perfect marketing ploy. Find Cane. Maybe create a conspiracy... If that's what you're doing... No company in the world would invest so much in a man and have no idea about him."

Her face went cold. She stood. "We told you before, Mr. Trent. This isn't a stunt. We don't need tricks to sell Cane's work. And what you are saying sounds delusional. Cane wrote in clues about faking his disappearance in every book. Why? Just to market another one?"

Trent raised his hands. "No offense. I happen to *deal* in tricks. I have no idea of *why* it is, I just sense it's not *what* you say. You see, I can see the connective strands, I just don't know where they go. And yeah, I may sound mad even suggesting it. But I have never been wrong before."

"Uh huh." She turned and started walking toward the hallway. "Now, if you don't mind, it's late. I have to be up early. You need to get some sleep too. A lot of sleep."

At the front door, she opened it and gestured for him to leave.

Trent sighed, grabbed the takeout, and stepped into the hall.

"I'll find him, you know that?" he said.

"We *want* you to," she replied. "Just don't see patterns in things that have none. And please, take a break from reading the books. They're obviously not good for your state of mind."

He paused at the threshold, glancing back. She shifted under his gaze. For a brief second, something thick hung in the air, not silence, but something more.

"Maybe you're right. Maybe it *is* the MSG," he said with a smile.

She slammed the door in his face.

Trent left Styles' apartment with the widest smirk. The cold city air bit against his face, but he barely cared. His mind was a churn of thoughts, and at the center of it, was her.

He had intended only one thing with that visit to Styles' apartment, to see a crack in her demeanor. To make sure he was on the right track before he started his research into Cane's work. He knew seeing Harlow tonight would have gotten him nothing, but Styles was not the closed book she thought she was. Yes, his theory was half-baked, but he needed her to know that he saw a flaw in the claim. And he wanted to see her reaction out of the safety of her office, and late at night when her defenses were unprepared.

It was satisfying when he saw that little twitch in her eyebrow, that flicker of something behind what she thought was her perfectly composed mask. A crack. A flinch. He had no idea if what he was saying was true, but he wanted to see her reaction. The reaction someone gets when they think you have found them out. And tonight, spouting what he did, he did just that.

She *was* hiding something, of that, he was now completely sure. Whatever little secret Arcane Publishing was sitting on, he was closer to it than she wanted him to be. And if she was that flustered already, well, it meant he wasn't wrong.

Did he believe that Cane really developed his own escape plan in his books? Who cares? What he did know was that Cane was *just* an author. His world was his novels. So, did Arcane get him to leave? Or did he tell them he couldn't meet the deadline, so concocted this to buy time?

Whatever it was Sutter Cane was not *missing*. Trent felt that in his bones, and he knew the books had something more to them than just overwrought descriptions and terrible melodrama.

Chuckling to himself, he zipped his jacket higher and descended into the subway, his shoes echoing off the steps as he went.

Styles stood at her window, watching the midnight city lit by nightlife. She clutched her telephone tightly to her ear.

The call rang on the other end. Once. Twice. Then—

"This better be good," Harglow's voice said, clipped and annoyed. Not the sound of a man who was asleep, but a man who was doing something.

"It's Linda," she said, sounding troubled. "John Trent's getting suspicious. He knows something isn't making sense."

There was a pause, and audible sigh from Harglow.

"He can't prove anything," he said. "Whatever he proposes, just go along with it. Everything will work out for the best."

And with that, the line went dead.

In The Mouth of Madness

The night passed into day, then to night and into day again, and John Trent was back on his couch, the morning light barely creeping through his closed blinds. He hadn't slept. Not really. Maybe he'd dozed off here and there, but he'd not moved from his position in the living room since seeing Styles. He had been looking deeper into Canes' work. Seeing if any of what he suggested had any legs or was just nonsense. Scribbling frantically into a notepad as he read through novel after novel, the nearby ashtray overflowed with the chain-smoked butts.

The coffee table in front of him was a chaotic mess of paperbacks. Cane's novels splayed out. All stacked, spread, pages torn out and scrawled upon. His notepad was a spiderweb of underlines, arrows, and scribbled annotations. He had gone very deep into the writing, but found little more than he had presented to Styles. It was frustrating. He felt there was more. He sensed it with every part of his body. But he found little else that could be a signpost, a clue.

His eyes were red-rimmed and dry. His hands jittered from too much caffeine, nicotine and not enough sleep. He threw the pen down in frustration and leaned back, rubbing his face, trying to massage some sense into him.

As he pulled his hands away, two black streaks of ink slashed across his cheeks like war paint. The pen had leaked, busted near the tip, bleeding cheap black liquid into his hands.

"Beautiful," he muttered.

He didn't move to clean it off. What was the point? He was too tired to care. Instead, he pulled a cigarette from the pack beside him and clicked the lighter. It flared up, but just before he lit the end, he paused.

Something was wrong.

He looked down.

He had the cigarette in backwards, filter first.

He was tired. Very tired.

He frowned, pulled it out, flipped it around, and lit it properly, dragging smoke into his lungs like it was the only thing that could keep him awake.

"Where the fuck did you go...?" he exhaled, eyes squinting at the paperbacks laid out before him.

There were two books in particular, side by side, seemingly innocuous, *The Thing in the Basement* and *The Breathing Tunnel*. Their covers faced upward. At first glance, they were just more of the same, lurid horror art, all shadows and teeth and vague shapes looming in subterranean spaces. But Trent noticed something else.

He leaned in closer. Peering past the art, and to the background of the covers.

The edges of some of the drawn lines met across the two covers like two pieces of a jigsaw. A jagged pipeline of shadow on one cover lined up perfectly with a distorted horizon on the other. It was subtle, no more than a clever design quirk, probably meant to sell more copies, but it was *so* exact. And suddenly, he realized it wasn't the only match. He looked at every other cover and they had the same background designs. Lines and dots in the background of the pictures. All that bled off the edges.

His eyes widened. He pulled a third book toward him. Turned it cover-side up. Then a fourth. Lining them up.

With one sudden, furious motion, he swept the notepad, the torn pages, his pens off the table in a chaotic flurry.

Leaving only his ashtray and the books in front of him.

Grabbing each book, he tore the covers off and cast the pages to one side, slamming each cover on the table in front of him. Turning and rearranging them together. Looking for the hidden pattern that lined up with the next image. Turning one cover upside down. Another on its side, until they all intersected. All as one pattern.

A ghostly shadow. The circle of monstrous kids. The church spire. The tentacles. They weren't the cover's purposes. They were just illustrations on top of the shapes *behind* them.

And when they were all together, he could see what that shape was.

It was a map.

A hidden pattern that made up a shape that looked like... a shape of a city? A state? And the dots... landmarks?

He stared at them for a while. Feeling as if he was looking at something only he had ever discovered. Why would this even be on the cover? If it was a map, did Sutter Cane want to be found? Was it just his posturing knowing the truth was out there and no one knew?

Somewhere, in the back of his mind, Trent heard the echo from his dream. Not a memory. Not quite. A whisper from a voice that wasn't his.

'He sees you.'

Chapter Four

In Harglow's office, the silence that hung between the three of them was not comfortable. It was taut, expectant.

With a loud *smack*, John Trent broke the silence.

He slammed a stack of glossy, oversized photographs onto the desk, images of Sutter Cane's book covers blown up to a larger size. He spread all six of them out across the table. Harglow's aged brow creased slightly as he peered at the images, as Styles, arms crossed and skeptical as ever, looked over at Trent somewhat pitifully.

"What is this?" Harglow asked, with an unimpressed twinge in his voice. "They're covers... I thought you said you cracked this wide open?"

Trent shook his head. "Don't look at them *individually*," he said, tapping one. "Look at them *together*."

Styles stepped closer, her curiosity vaguely piqued.

Her gaze darted from one image to the next, scanning them.

Trent grinned with satisfaction as he recognized the confusion. "Okay, I'll make it easier."

He reached into the folder beside the table and produced another sheet, all six covers pieced together in his discovered jigsaw pattern. The outlines cut around the map pattern he had discovered. In all, it was now a single shape.

Styles' breath caught for a moment. "It's a map?" she whispered in some amazement.

"Now you get it," Trent said.

"A map of what?" Harglow asked. "Hobb's End?"

"Think so," Trent nodded, "That's why Cane insisted on doing the artwork himself. It wasn't just to doodle a stupid monster on the cover."

He reached into the folder and produced another sheet, a transparent overlay, glossy and thin. Upon it, drawn in precise lines and faint labels, was a map of New England.

"Watch this," he said.

Carefully, Trent laid the transparent sheet over the composite of the covers. The effect was instantaneous. The chaotic art, the grotesque townscapes, the horror-infused sketches... they aligned perfectly.

The crooked street in *The Feeding* curved seamlessly into the withered highway in *The Thing in the Basement*. The lopsided steeple of *The Hobb's End Horror* nestled into the distorted skyline from *The*

Breathing Tunnel. All of them came together, to form the complete, unmistakable map.

"Do you see?" Trent said, his voice electric with triumph. "Hobb's End isn't on *any* official map. It's not the name of a real place. We know that. But look... These lines match up. That highway there? That bend in the river? All match with real-world geography. The dots? They are cities in the state... and here." He pointed to one part that had what looked like a red X in the image. "Here is where Hobb's End is. Or whatever name it has outside of the books. Like it or not, Cane's covers put Hobb's End slap bang in the middle of New England."

Styles looked over the covers closely. "What town is there really?"

"Now that's the fun part," Trent shrugged. "There isn't one. Not on any map I could find. It's just a space. It doesn't exist. He invented it there."

"You're saying Cane went someplace ... fictional?" Harglow asked, his voice almost worried.

"No. I'm saying it's real," Trent replied. "A real place. In a real state. Just not on any map. I think he was fucking with the readers. Showing them where it was. And I just *know* he is gonna be there."

Harglow scoffed quietly. "This isn't the gold rush. All towns and cities are mapped, aren't they?"

"America's got plenty of ghost towns it's forgotten," Trent said. "Little pockets of nowhere that were abandoned and died out..."

"How can you be so sure he's there?" Harglow asked.

"I'm not," Trent replied. "But I need to go to be sure... Look at his writing. He loves being a puppet master. Controlling the reader. This seems like move he would make, doesn't it? You know him."

Styles looked at Harglow.

Trent spoke quieter, just between the three of them. "And you're *sure* you still want me to find him?"

Harglow didn't answer immediately. He sat back, arms crossed, glancing at the map. "We have nothing to hide, Mr. Trent," he eventually said. "All we desire is what we're owed. If Cane is dead, we want our fair share. If he's alive, we want our property." He motioned toward Styles. "Go with my blessing. I'm sure you won't mind if Linda accompanies you on this expedition?"

Trent looked at Styles with a polite grin, the kind that said he was already imagining the uncomfortable road trip ahead of them. "I'm gonna be plain about this," he said. "I believe you knew more about this than you're saying. And I will find it out."

I know what you're thinking as you read this.

Why is he talking to me? Why is Sutter Cane breaking into his story and speaking at this moment? Right at a key moment of decision?

Maybe I'm not.

Maybe I'm just thinking out loud, or... maybe you're eavesdropping.

Doesn't matter.

Some people like their stories neat. Beginning, middle, end. But you have read my other books, correct? You know they tend to leak a little.

They are not cut and dry comfortable tales.

This isn't about what the story is.

That's not the question.

Not yet.

Keep going.

* * *

As the sun began to set, Trent's rental car crossed the Union Port bridge, on its way out of New York, heading north toward Maine. Usually an eight-hour drive, but because of highway closures and diversions around Vermont, the journey would take closer to sixteen hours, and being the time of day it was, meant he and Styles would need to split the driving throughout the night.

Styles sat stiffly on the passenger seat, her belt pulled tight. Every sharp turn, every burst of acceleration made her hands grip the door handle a little bit harder. Trent was not a safe driver in her eyes. He was erratic, short-tempered, New York driver through and through, and as he drove, and invariably got more annoyed at everyone else on the road, his Brooklyn accent came out stronger as he hurled loud insults at them.

"Can you please slow down?" she asked, trying to sound calm, but failing.

"Slow?" Trent laughed. "This is New York, this *is* slow,"

"Please...," was all she managed to reply, as the car sped around a corner, and she gripped the seat tighter.

"I gotta grab a smoke," Trent said, already leaning forward. "Here, take the wheel."

"*What?*"

As he let go, Styles reached over and caught the wheel, startled. Her knuckles turned white as she gripped.

"I can't drive like this," she gasped in a panic.

"You'd never know," Trent replied, lighting up, unfazed. "You're a natural."

With a chuckle, Trent pressed down on the gas pedal as the car veered across lanes. Horns blared around them in anger.

Terrified, Styles held onto the wheel like it might come off in her hands.

Trent soon took back over. "You need to calm down, Styles. Just relax."

"I don't *need* to relax, I just need you to *not* kill us, is that too much to ask?"

"And I need you to tell me the truth, and admit

that Arcane knows more... But we can't have everything we want now, can we?"

By the time midnight passed, the landscape had changed, and the erratic driving had quelled. The bright neon lights of the city were long gone, as was the battle of traffic. The roads here were wider, lined with dark fields and empty stretches of nothing. No other cars. No lights around them. Only their headlights lit their way along this two-lane blacktop.

Trent was still at the wheel. Styles had drifted off, her head turned toward the window. He was glancing down at the map spread across his lap, trying to make sense of it as he drove. But the road he was on was not the road he thought it was. What should be veering right, was now curving to the left. Where he should have passed Farmington, there was nothing out of the window.

Shit.

He was lost, very lost... and he knew it was all his fault. He was sure he would be fine with no map. He had great navigation skills, well, he thought he had. But after the seventh hour of being on the road, when the night set in deeply, every road now looked the same. Nothing but night and asphalt.

After a few seconds, he gave up, crumpled the map on his lap, and tossed it over his shoulder into the backseat.

He needed Styles. He needed another pair of eyes on this.

A mischievous smile quickly appeared on his face as he had a thought. Looking at her, at how peaceful she looked, he wondered if he should, or if it was being too immature...

Before considering any real ramifications, he gingerly leaned across and opened the glove compartment. There on the top of the car's registration documents was a small air horn, the sort that belonged at cheap stadiums and frat parties. Something he had bought years ago and never had a call to use.

He looked at her, asleep and peaceful, took a breath, then blew it full blast.

The noise bellowed throughout the car.

Trent tossed the horn into the back seat right before she jolted awake with a scream.

"We're lost," he said, acting as if nothing had happened.

She regarded him, stunned, but she was not fooled. She could still hear the ringing in her ears.

With a grunt of annoyance, she reached down to her feet and picked up a half-crushed bag of chips and started hitting him with it.

"You couldn't just shake me?" she shouted. "You asshole!"

Potato chips flew out of the bad like confetti, all over Trent.

"Alright! Enough!" Trent said, shielding himself as

he could not contain his laughter. "Even Steven! Truce! Truce! I just need help with directions... I think we're lost. Need you to look out, looking for any landmarks or towns. Okay?"

She dropped the bag back to her footwell, picked a large chip off Trent's shoulder, and popped it into her mouth.

"Fine, but I'll say it again, Hobb's End *doesn't* exist, and even if Cane based it on a town around here, it means nothing." she said. "So, you're gonna be driving round here all night, looking for ghosts."

Trent smiled. "I just got a feeling about it. And my feelings never steer me wrong."

"A tingling?" she asked with some sarcasm.

The further they drove, the stranger the night felt. The outside seemed too quiet. The land was too empty. There were no road signs. There were no pit stops. The sky was filled with too many stars. It started to feel like they were driving in part of an unchartered country, not what should be the middle of rural Maine.

Trent, realizing that the air horn may have been a step too childish, tried to keep things light as they went on. "So, you really like working on Cane's stuff, huh?"

"Sure. You really like busting people?" she shot back.

"I like catching frauds and phonies. Watching people get caught in their own lies? Yeah, I love it. It's satisfying... 'Cause so many people in this world are trying to scam somebody else. Rip them off. And I'm just the guy who turns the lights on. I don't like liars... And the best part, I like it when the shit goes sour, and they realize they have run out of bullshit to tell."

"How admirable," she said, dryly.

"Anyway, we were talking about *you*." Trent smirked. "How did you get hooked up with Cane in the first place?"

"I've been a fan of horror books since high school. Especially Lovecraft and King... I like being scared. And I was working at Arcane when Cane's first book, *The Thing in the Basement,* came out. And it... It scared me. I fought to work with him, and by the time *The Feeding* was released, I'd proven myself to Harglow enough, that he trusted me to take it on. Especially after his last editor had quit. His writing terrifies me more than anything I've ever experienced."

He gave her a look. "It terrifies you? Even though it's not real? I get spooked, but terrified?"

"It's not real from your point of view, and right now, reality happens to share your point of view. What scares me about Cane's work is what might happen if reality shared his point of view."

"What's that supposed to mean?" Trent kept one eye on the road. "How can reality share a fictional point of view?"

"Reality is nothing more than what we tell it to be. Sane and insane could easily switch positions if the insane were to become the majority. Think politics. Nazis were not always in power. But the reality of what was right and wrong shifted to allow them to."

"So, for Cane, you think everyone *could* believe in monsters and that suddenly they would just spring to life?"

Styles shook her head with a smile. "Look at most horror stories. Normal people encounter monstrous things. Battle said monstrous things. Cane's stories are not about that. They are about people becoming monstrous, granted literally. But you could take his works and apply them metaphorically to anything. His books are about sane becoming insane. And when you realize that, you realize how terrifying his stories truly are."

"Huh... I," Trent hated to say it. "I can't lie, I never thought of that while reading, but I guess you got a point."

"Sanity's just a consensus. If the majority went mad, the sane would be the ones locked up wondering what happened to the world. You'd be on your own in a world full of madness."

Trent didn't respond right away. Her words hung in the air, a little too heavy for comfort.

"That is a fucking terrifying thought," he said, quieter than before. "Don't think I'd allow myself to get locked up, though."

"If you don't follow the new order, you would," she said. "If you realized that everything you've ever known was gone, you'd want to be as far away from the world as possible... if you didn't have the nerve to end it yourself."

Trent stared ahead, the road narrowing under the beams of his headlights.

"And you like to read that?"

"I like the idea, just like I like the idea of vampires or zombies. Doesn't have to be real to scare you, you just need the imagination to see how it *could* be real, the metaphor and allegory of it all," she said. "And sixty million other people agree with me."

As the night wore on, and Trent felt the exhaustion creeping in, Styles took over the driving duties. And before he fell asleep, Trent agreed to a pact, if there was nothing found by morning, they would turn back and go home. The further they got, the more Trent started to doubt his intuition. Had he believed the fiction too much? Had he succumbed to the reality that Cane had created? They say Cane's writing affects people, and he wondered, did it have an effect on him?

Styles stared out the windscreen, trying to see more of what lay ahead. The road had changed from two wide lanes, to a narrower set. The stars in the sky had also disappeared, hidden beneath dark clouds. She sighed as she lifted her hand to flick on her high beams, hoping that the extra illumination would keep her focused.

In The Mouth of Madness

As the road lit up, something moved within its beam, coming toward them.

A boy on a bicycle, pedaling as fast as his small legs could move rode in the opposite direction. His shape blurred for a second in the headlights, then passed. Styles stared into the rearview, watching him disappear into the darkness.

There *had* to be a town around here, she thought. Somewhere they could stop. Get a bite. Go to the toilet... She scanned the distance, looking for any sight of life. Any lights in the black.

Seconds then minutes passed, and nothing. There was nothing out there. No town. No village. No gas station. She barely noticed the thin fog that had started to gather along the edges of the windows. Slowly filling up the outside as it snaked along the road. Covering the asphalt slowly.

By the time she had noticed, the window was steaming up.

"What the—" she mumbled, as she reached her hand out to wipe the condensation away. As she did, her vision started to blur.

Then... movement again.

A figure ahead.

She tried to blink away the blur as she wiped at the glass with the palm of her hand.

She may not have seen clearly, but she could have sworn as he approached that it was somehow the same boy, passing them again.

Yet as he frantically rode by, she caught a clearer look at his face.

He may have had the same clothes and rode the same bike, but this person was old and gnarled. His hair was bone-white, his eyes wracked with terror. Yet still, he pedaled at speed, vanishing into the night behind them.

She rubbed her eyes.

"Oh my God..."

She *had* to have been mistaken. *It's just tiredness*, she tried to convince herself.

Trent stirred in the passenger seat, woken by her words.

"What's up?" he said.

"I saw... I saw a—" she could not finish her thought. She just looked around, blinking harder, as her vision remained blurry.

Trent peered around as well, trying to see what she had seen. "What was it? A town? A cow? What?"

She looked unsure. Unsure of her own eyes. "Never mind. It was nothing. I'm just tired I guess."

"Okay," he said, closing his eyes again, ready to drift back off. "Wake me if you see that nothing again."

She didn't reply. She just kept her eyes on the road. Continually rubbing at them, blinking, trying to stay focused. Ignoring the mist that was now coming in thicker.

She *had* to concentrate. She *had* to drive on. She just had to...

In The Mouth of Madness

...The boy was there again.

Not in the other lane.

Right in front of the car.

She screamed as she slammed on the brakes. The tires screamed as the car skidded sideways.

The rear of the vehicle spun outward, clipping the boy's bike, sending him spiraling through the air, landing hard on the road behind them.

Trent shot upright, but by the time he realized what had happened, Styles was already out of the car.

"I just hit a boy!" she shouted.

"Oh, shit," Trent muttered, scrambling out of his seat.

They ran toward the boy. His body lay sprawled on the road, motionless in a heap. A few feet away his bike lay bent by the collision. The wheels buckled in on themselves, the spokes all snapped outward.

Styles stood with her hand over her mouth. Scared. Upset. Horrified.

Trent crouched, reaching for the boy, who was lying face down, groaning painfully.

Trent did not see the young boy, but had expected one as he gently rolled him over.

But the boy's skin was like that of someone in their nineties. Wrinkled and grey, with a bulbous nose and elongated ears, he looked as if an old man's face had been grafted on a small boy's body. It didn't just look wrong, it looked unnatural. The boy's hands and arms were smooth and youthful, same for his legs that poked out beneath his shorts.

Blood trickled from both of his aged nostrils, down his lip and cheeks.

His eyes moved, trying to focus as he looked up at Trent. As he spoke, his voice was trembling. "I can't get out. It won't let me."

Styles still stood in shock, not believing what she had done.

Trent turned to her, about to ask her to help him pick the boy up to get him into the car, but before he could, she staggered back in shock. Looking behind him.

Turning, Trent's blood ran just as cold, as there, sat on his bike—the bike that had been ruined—was the boy. Staring back at them helplessly.

There was no blood from his nose.

The bike was how it had been.

Not a stitch out of place.

Before either of them could say a thing, the old boy pedaled away down the dark road, faster than seemed possible.

"He—He's okay," Trent said, standing up, staring into the blackness where the boy raced off into. Trying to make sense of it all. "He's just not hurt. He got up."

Styles was shaking. "No. He's *not* okay, you saw him... The bike... it was totaled."

"Obviously not," he replied, not sounding sure.

"You saw his face! You *saw* it!"

In The Mouth of Madness

There was no way that Trent could accept what he thought he saw.

Neither of them said more as they got back in the car.

The sun had started its slow crawl into the sky, casting a dull orange across the horizon. It wasn't warm yet. Just brought an empty light, pouring it across the narrow road, dissolving the darkness it could reach.

Dust drifted lazily around the car as it came to a stop on the hilltop. The engine clicked over, cooling down after carrying them too many miles.

They hadn't seen another soul since that gas station in Glenburn. No towns. No motels. Not even any signs. Just road. Nothing... except for that boy. That one strange boy on the bike, with a face that didn't belong to his body. Though the sun had started to rise, and the land seemed a million miles away from the thickness of the night that the boy pedaled into, that all only happened twenty minutes ago.

Even with the sunrise, there was still nothing. The darkness hadn't been hiding a thing.

Trent stood at the front of the car, elbows on the hood, the map spread out in front of him. His eyes scanned it again. He looked at it like it might suddenly give him the answer if he stared hard enough.

"It's not here," he muttered. "This road makes no damn sense."

Now, in the pale sunrise, Styles was standing a little way off, at the edge of the hill. She hadn't said a word since they stopped. Arms folded, her eyes fixed on something in the distance. The wind pushed her hair across her face, but she didn't move. Just stood there.

"What was the last town we passed?" Trent asked, not expecting an answer.

Still nothing from her.

He sighed and jabbed a finger down at the map. "This is the X. Two hundred and sixty-two miles after Bangor. That's what it should be. That's what the odometer says. We *should* be there."

His voice was more exasperated than angry. His whole plan had seemingly unraveled. He thought it should be here. Something should be here.

"We passed nothing! Not a *goddamn* thing! We could be in Bumfuck, Idaho, and I wouldn't know the difference."

Styles didn't move. She was distracted. Still. Staring at the valley intently.

He looked up. "Styles?"

He folded the map with a sharp, deliberate motion. "I give in. Cane's full of shit. This whole trip was bullshit. Happy?" Noticing the pained expression on her face his tone altered. "Hey," he said gently. "You alright?"

She didn't answer. Her brow was furrowed, eyes squinting into the distance. Her hand hovered at the side of her head, fingers lightly pressing her temple. She looked pale. Unsteady.

"What is it?" he asked again.

"I thought... I saw something," she said quietly.

Trent turned, followed her gaze.

There was nothing.

Just grassland sloping down into a wide, empty valley. Some trees. Low, rolling hills beyond. All of it bathed in a bright early light, still quiet. Still empty.

"There's nothing there," he said, shading his eyes. "Just—"

A pain hit without warning. A hot, stabbing line behind his eyes, like someone driving nails through the base of his skull. He stumbled back half a step, hand snapping up to his face.

"Jesus—"

It wasn't just a pain. It was pressure. Like his brain was trying to swell past the confined of his skull.

His vision blurred. And as it did the light in front of him changed. Or maybe the air did. He couldn't tell which. It shimmered. Contorted. Like heat rising off pavement, but different.

And through that shimmer, he saw it.

Like the landscape had peeled back a layer.

Lines sharpened. Shapes bled into focus. A row of rooftops. A fence. A bridge. An entire town, nestled into the valley.

Trent's heart was hammering. The pain dulled but

didn't vanish. He forced himself to look back there again.

The town was there.

"What the hell..." he whispered.

Beside him, Styles finally spoke again, her voice a thin wire.

"You see it now?" she said, shaken. "I felt it too."

Trent rubbed his eyes. It didn't help. The image wouldn't go away.

"This is some kind of trick," he muttered. "Light, or... or something. A mirage. Some kind of—"

The words drifted away. This was too confusing.

He opened the car door and climbed in without another word. His hands shook as he gripped the wheel.

Styles followed.

"What's going on, Trent?" she asked. "It wasn't there when I first looked. I *know* it wasn't..."

He didn't look at her.

"We'll figure it out," he said. His voice was calm, but it wasn't bravado.

Whatever just happened, the shimmering of light, the pain in his head, the town suddenly being there, it didn't change the fact that he'd been right. They'd found the place that he *knew* was there.

Maybe that should've scared him more.

But it didn't.

Not yet.

Chapter Five

Welcome to Hobb's End – The Heart of America. That's what the sign said, sat on the edge of the town. The foliage around it was overgrown, positioned next to an old wooden covered bridge across a creek into what looked like the main street through the town.

Trent had stopped the car beside it and could only stare. Half amazed, half confused.

"It's actually called Hobb's End?" he asked, struggling to find the words.

Styles kept looking around them, through every window, expecting it to be some kind of elaborate joke.

They drove over the bridge, and as the wood under the tires turned back to stone, and they faced up the wide drag through the quaint town, Trent looked into the rearview once, then again, and then a third time, as if what they'd driven over might not be there when he looked back, he'd glimpse any movement of people, hiding away, wanting not to be seen. The architects of the ruse.

The main street through the town was quiet. And it was not what either of them expected. It looked abandoned. The hand-painted signs that hung from partially boarded-up shop doorways were weather-beaten. Their lettering faded by rain, sun and time, but still barely readable. An antique shop. A barber. A drugstore. It looked like a usual small-town, but without life.

Autumnal leaves drifted on the wind ahead of them, along with some old newspaper and assorted trash. The windows on the buildings not smashed or boarded were filthy and dusty.

Styles' hands rested tensely on her knees, as she stared around. Her eyes looked at everything with recognition and disbelief tangled.

"It's exactly how he described it," she muttered.

Trent felt the same. The memory of the books were still fresh in his mind.

He had expected to find something. But to find *this*? A ghost town of what he had read? He did not expect that at all.

As he slowed the car, he looked in passing doorways. In windows. Hoping to see some hole in the story.

In The Mouth of Madness

Up ahead, in the road, some cars had been abandoned, sat near the curbs like husks, their windows cracked. One had its door flung wide open. Another had been rammed into a storefront at some point, its nose now buried in a display of mannequins that slumped in the melee of glass and brick.

"Here's as good a place as any," Trent said, finally pulling to a stop behind one of the cars. "Shall we go find your author?"

Styles was still looking out the window, still not believing any of this was real.

Getting out, Trent looked around at the surrounding buildings, looking to see a person. A CCTV camera. Instead, he noticed something he could not see from the driver's seat. The angles of the architecture here were askew. Nothing was truly at a right angle. The corners didn't quite meet ninety degrees. The window frames leaned ever so slightly. Gutters jutted at almost imperceptible off angles just enough to unsettle the eye. Everything was a few degrees off, and when he noticed that, it made the whole town appear surreal.

"There's no birds," Styles said.

She was right. Trent listened and could not hear a thing either.

They started walking up the street.

"I guess we missed a big party," he said grimly. "Looks like everyone just left this place... You hear about that in Pennsylvania? The one with the coal mine fire that wouldn't go out? Maybe everyone was evacuated like there?" He suddenly looked concerned. "We better be careful, okay?"

Styles was not listening. She had stopped walking and looked back, her head to one side. Listening.

She heard it again, faint but unmistakable.

Laughter.

High-pitched. Light. Children.

She opened her eyes, her stare snapping down the street. A few blocks down, a group of young children were chasing an emaciated dog into an adjacent alley.

"Look, there!" she said.

Trent turned, just as the last child had disappeared.

"What?" he asked.

"You didn't see them? Or hear them?" She pointed. "Down there. There were kids."

Trent saw nothing. He heard nothing. He just saw a dead street in a dead town.

"Are you sure?" he asked.

"I..." Styles did not know for sure *what* she saw. Not here. "Forget it... I... I don't know."

He waited a beat. "Let's just carry on, if you see them again, we'll go have a look, okay?"

It wasn't that Trent didn't believe she saw something, but he could not trust her word. He still thought that she had something to do with all of this. That it was some kind of crazy stunt... Maybe it was an

In The Mouth of Madness

opening of Sutter Cane Land or something equally as dumb. Actually, that could explain this being here... Get an investigator to find it. Announce to the world. Would explain the badly made buildings that were not all straight. But the pain on the hill... Did she drug him? He would consider all of that later, but one thing he would not do, follow her lead. He would not do what was expected if she was part of a set up.

Styles straightened and took a breath. "This place isn't right?"

"No shit, none of it's right."

"Everything is exactly how it was written. Like I know the hotel is up the street over there. I know that Deakin's hardware is on the corner right ahead... I saw those kids running across the road, so where did they come from? Only one place they could have been. From the school. The school I know is just down there... I know this place. I know it like I lived here."

"I read the books too. Didn't seem that specific. Sure, I recognized the store names. But none of his books have the town like this do they?"

Styles shrugged. "There was a fan who sent in a map of the town. They went through every description in every book and worked out where the buildings should be, where the homes were. There was some guess work for sure... But I got that map on the wall of my office. It's... *this*."

"Okay, and you saw kids I didn't see. So, what do we do with all of that?"

Styles had no answers. She glanced up at an attic window that sat three floors up. "That window at the top there? That's where the girl hung herself in the opening of *The Feeding*."

Trent looked at the name of the store beneath, Red Hook Haberdashery. He remembered this too. He remembered in detail. He hadn't taken in much of that book, but that bit had disturbed him. The way the character's feet had kicked against the attic window, and all the townsfolk waited for it to happen. Then what they did to her after...

He quoted a line from the book that had stuck with him... "Meat that murders itself is the best meat to eat".

He didn't like how easily that came back to him.

Before he could form anything resembling a counterargument, she pointed again, this time at a rusted bike leaning against a lamppost. Its tires were flat. Its chain had broken and was now coiling to the ground.

"Chapter seven of *The Breathing Tunnel*," she said. "The boy has that accident on his bike and leaves it here before he goes underground and gets eaten. Remember that?"

"So, what is this? You think Cane put all this here?"

"No," she said. "Yes... I dunno... Maybe?"

He looked either way up the street, then back to the car.

"Let's get our bags and go to the hotel. Even if it's empty like the rest of this place, we can find a bed to crash in for the night... We can regroup after we rest up, deal?"

There it stood.

Three stories tall. Faded green siding. Flaking paint. A wrought iron sign that swung lazily from a crooked pole: The Pickman Hotel.

Trent stared up at it, an overnight bag in his hand.

The building stood squat and imposing, despite the painted yellow sun on the sign.

He remembered this place from the books, but the books were fiction. Sensationalist pulp. Horror for the masses.

The fact it was here meant one of two things; it was built based on the descriptions in the book, or the book was just describing this place. He did not know which version of that he preferred.

Have you ever walked into a room and felt like you were being watched?

Not by someone, but some... thing.

A presence. An intrusive thought not from your own creation?

Most people shrug those things off. Goosebumps, bad lighting, low blood sugar, other discountable heebie jeebies.

But that feeling? That unease?

It's just a welcoming. Spoken in another tongue that you cannot hear.

An embrace of sorts.

An embrace that is forever.

When you feel it... embrace it back.

* * *

It was the musty smell that hit first.

Walking in, Trent was immediately reminded of his grandmother's old apartment in Yonkers. A small place filled with frilly tablecloths, ornamental dolls and plates on the wall. A home filled with items whose purpose seemed to just gather dust and mold. And *that* smell that came with it. One of dust and aging laced with nicotine... and like there, here it was too. Filling up the foyer of this small provincial building. The smell was in the carpets, the thick drapes. Everywhere.

Whatever life or bustle or charm the building once had held was now laying in rot. There was no lobby music, no chime of a welcoming bell over the door, no murmur of guests or shuffling of staff. Just a stale smell that hung in the air like the dried cobwebs that caked the corner of the room.

Despite its dilapidated condition, it was still somewhat quaint. The wallpaper was a faded floral print that was a bit too garish for modern-day establishments to be brave enough to have. The thick net curtains blocked most of the sunlight from getting in, and they had hidden something that surprised Trent, there were lights on in here. He would have bet his life that no one was here. But the lights said otherwise.

The front desk sat to the right, all wood with brass trim, dulled with time and neglect.

Styles followed, shutting the door behind her. Without looking around, she closed her eyes as she tried her best to remember.

"There should be three paintings behind us," she said, more to herself than to Trent. "Pastoral scenes. Peaceful. I think one has a couple walking by a creek?"

Trent turned toward the wall behind them.

And there they were.

Three paintings, framed in thin gold-painted wood, hung in perfect alignment above a dusty green couch. They looked just as she had described. Pastoral and peaceful. The first was of a herd of cows grazing in a sun-dappled field. The second showed a young boy mid-laugh, caught in the act of throwing a stick for a small black dog leaping beside him. The third depicted a young couple strolling beside a creek under a large weeping willow. All three were soft and impressionistic. Calming. Charming. Harmless. Yet still quite bland and neutered.

"You've got a better memory for Cane's detail than I do," Trent said. "And I only read them over the last couple of days." He found nothing surprising about this. More acting from Styles. Perfectly executed.

Styles turned and saw the paintings. She didn't look too happy that she was right. She looked more concerned. "I've been living these stories for a while. I must have read each book at least a dozen times."

"Surprised you don't have an axe ready," Trent smirked.

"That's not funny," she replied, unimpressed.

Seeing the bad taste of his comment, he held his hands up. "Sorry."

As they walked toward the front desk, Styles suddenly reached out and grabbed Trent's arm, stopping him mid-step.

"Watch it," she said quietly. "The boards are loose there."

Trent raised an eyebrow. He tapped the spot with the toe of his shoe. Sure enough, the floorboard shifted slightly under the pressure, creaking with a tired groan.

He looked at her. "That's in the book too?"

Another trick, he thought.

But she didn't answer. She didn't have time, as the service bell on the desk dinged loudly, echoing through the room. Grabbing their attention.

They both turned and saw that behind the desk stood an old woman, who had just rung her own service bell to get their attention. She was small and seemed extremely happy to see them. She carried with her a comforting vibe. With her white hair in a neat bun, frilly print, she carried the gentle stoop of someone who'd spent a lifetime baking pies and tending to flower beds. Her face was a vision of warm pleasantries.

"Can I help you folks?" the old lady asked, her voice sugar-sweet and crooning.

Trent suddenly turned on the charm, all smiles and relaxed posture. "Sure hope so, ma'am," he said. "Me and the missus here are headed to Boston. Thought we'd take a break in your little famous hometown."

The woman's smile flickered.

"Famous?" she asked, as she handed him a pen and pushed an old-fashioned ledger toward him. "Hobb's End is famous now?"

"Sure, with that whole Sutter Cane thing and all." He looked down at the ledger and signed his name.

Styles had returned to stare at the paintings on the wall. Her expression was confused and troubled.

"Sutter who?" the old lady asked.

"I heard he was from around here. No? Comes back to visit?"

The old lady shook her head, slow and deliberate. "Don't know anybody named that," she said. "Nobody passes through here much anymore. Let me get your keys."

"Could we get two rooms please?" Trent quickly added.

The old lady turned, puzzled as she nodded.

"You need a deposit?" Trent asked.

The woman froze and quickly laughed. It started

as a chuckle, then bloomed into full-bodied laughter. It was far too loud and went on for far too long.

"City folk..." she wheezed, wiping her eyes. "I'll get you rooms nine and ten, is that okay?"

"My lucky number's nine, so great for me!"

The old lady turned and disappeared into the office.

"Well, she's a character," mumbled under his breath.

But Styles didn't answer.

She was still fixed on the paintings.

She could not look away... Because one of the cows had changed position.

Only a little. Just a twitch. The barest hint of motion.

But it *had* moved.

Hadn't it?

Trent dropped his bag onto the floor of bedroom number nine. It landed with a thud and he immediately turned on Styles, aggravated. "We are *not* living inside a damn Sutter Cane story," he snapped, having been listening to her paranoia all the way up the stairs. A paranoia he thought was fake.

"This *town* is all his," she protested. "Everything here is. You see that clear as day."

Trent huffed. "No," he jabbed a finger toward the

town outside the window. "The town *inspired* the stories. Not the other way around."

Styles didn't answer him. She just reached into her bag and pulled out a familiar paperback, *The Hobb's End Horror*.

"This place. Each building. That woman downstairs. They're all in here," she said, holding the book up.

Trent let out a hollow laugh. "The Mrs. Pickman in the book is a lunatic. She chops her husband into goddamn coleslaw," he said. "The woman we met downstairs? I'd bet her idea of violence is soaking her dentures in her husband's beer."

"And in that book, it was exactly how she was written. Even after she killed him. Remember the guests having no idea. Even when she changed into that thing. They still couldn't believe it. Until she killed them?"

"How come she's not a monster now then?" Trent countered. "If it's real. If this is Cane's book that we've magicked into somehow. Then she should have a hundred tentacles and have destroyed the hotel. Right? She should be attacking the whole town. The buildings would be burned down after the people defended themselves. But no, she's a little old dear, cute as a button and not one tentacle in sight. Or have I got that part of the book wrong?... You can't pick and choose your argument here. Either it's all what Cane wrote or it's just circumstantial and he based everything on this town."

Styles didn't laugh. "Trent..." she said, her voice shaking now. "What if Cane's work isn't fiction? What if he's been a reporter this whole time? Telling the story of this town, what he saw."

That proposition made Trent look at her as if she had lost her mind.

"And before you say I'm going crazy, we both saw this town just appear out of thin fucking air."

He turned to a small wooden side table and rapped it sharply with his knuckles "You want a report?" he said. "*This* is reality." He knocked on it again. "Hear that? *Reality*. And besides, if what you're saying is true, if this is *really* a Sutter Cane story, then, just as in that book, the guest sees a big black Byzantine church out the window. And it has got an upside-down cross right on the steeple, correct? You think that just happens to be in this town as well? Did you see it? No. You wanna know why? 'Cause some things Cane *had* to invent, or every story would be dull Americana. Not monsters in the shadows and killer grandmas."

He moved to the nearest window, gripped the curtain, and yanked it open. The view overlooked a collection of small houses. A curve of trees shimmered in the distance. It was a scene devoid of any malice.

"See?" he said, gesturing as if he had won. "*Reality*. Not those bullshit stories."

Styles didn't rise to the anger. She slowly walked to

the other side of the room, toward the opposite-facing window.

"You didn't read closely enough," she said, nervously. "The view from the hotel room was from the east."

Her hand slipped into the curtain. Drew it aside.

The church was there, slap bang in the middle of the town.

Not a quaint country chapel or some steepled postcard. No. This thing came out of a nightmare. Made of black stone, scabbed with age. The architecture was pointed. Vicious. Its steeple stood up like a dagger, and on top of it, unmistakable even from this distance... was a huge, inverted crucifix.

Trent didn't say a word. He couldn't.

Styles turned to look out of the window, the book still clutched in her hands. She didn't have to, as she *knew* it was going to be there. She *felt* it was going to be there. But she had to confirm her suspicions. She turned to the paperback in her hand, and rifled inside it, looking for a page.

Trent walked nearer, not sure what he was looking at, and not believing it could even be possible.

Styles read aloud from an open page. "This place had once been the seat of an evil older than mankind... and wider than the known universe. The cross on it hung upside down, not as an insult to the God of Abraham, but as a statement of inversion. Of what was not, now being. And what was, now dying."

He looked out of the window.

The black church, just as it appeared on the book cover.

He could not explain this. Would they have built this as well? Just for the ruse? It looked immense... and old. Very old. Yet he did not see it before. Surely it could be seen from every street corner? From up on that hill?

His mind spun with trying to rationalize it all.

Maybe it was all a theme park?

Maybe it was a set for a film?

Maybe this is just the town he lived, and that is... that is...

His head hurt trying to figure it out.

The sky had turned from being sun-filled into a grey smear. The heat of the day had turned off in the short time they were inside the hotel. The streets had filled with an autumnal breeze, as a gloom settled on Hobb's End.

Trent walked ahead, the dog-eared *Hobb's End Horror* paperback was clutched in one hand, as he flicked through the pages. Styles followed him close behind, but her eyes never stayed in one place for long. She kept glancing behind them, as if expecting something to lurch after them. And in her mind, in this place, something just might.

"You've got me reading this thing like it's a fucking

In The Mouth of Madness

guidebook," he muttered, but there was no bite in his voice. The snark was still there, but it was more confused.

Styles' expression said enough of what she didn't say aloud. She could tell that something was wrong here, that something was about to happen. Even if she did not know what, even if was not written in the books, she just felt it. She just wished she could convince Trent. Not that she was surprised he had so many reservations about her and this place.

From a few blocks behind them, movement and a running of feet.

This time Trent noticed too, as he and Styles glanced behind them.

Those children again. Laughing, but their voices now sounded distorted. The joy there had been replaced with undertones of hysteria.

The children darted across the road, chasing something emaciated and shuffling across the ground. A dog? Maybe. But there seemed to be a couple of legs too many. From their vantage point, it was hard to see any of it clearly.

"This fucking place," Trent said with a shake of his head. "I bet he's having a damn good laugh at our expense..." He paused. "Okay, let's go building to building. Find anyone, ask about Cane. Someone's gotta say something, right? Not like they can all pretend they haven't heard of him."

It clicked. For Styles anyway. She remembered

what this was. "You'll have someone to ask in a few seconds," she said quietly.

He didn't have time to ask what she meant, as tires screamed on the concrete, as a roaring tore through the town like a furious lion. A battered station wagon came hurtling around the corner, skidding sideways in a spray of smoke.

Trent and Styles stepped back from the street and onto the sidewalk as the car barreled past them, not slowing, not braking, heading straight to the top of town... to the black church.

Trent felt that following them was playing along... But he had to see.

"Come on," he said, hurrying up the hill, after the car.

"Trent, wait!" she called out as she followed. But he did not want to listen.

Just short of the rusted fence that ringed the decaying yard to the black church, the station wagon ground to a halt.

All four doors slammed open, as eight men piled out, tense and shaking. Half of them carried shotguns, the others pistols. Each held them too tight. These were not violent men. They were *desperate* men, convincing themselves that they were capable of what they were doing. There was a feat in their movements and something worse behind their eyes. Not any form

In The Mouth of Madness

of insanity or rage, but grief. Each of them looked distraught.

The largest of them, a bearded man with a thick neck and wild eyes, stepped forward, cupped his hands around his mouth, and bellowed toward the towering, gothic mass of dark stone that loomed over them.

"Caaaaaaane!" he screamed, his voice cracking through the silent day.

A dozen feet back, Trent and Styles had caught up. They stopped and stared. That name. That *name*.

Trent remembered what Styles had just said. He turned to her, his voice edged with accusation.

"How did you know?" he demanded.

She didn't answer, she could only stare at the armed men at the church. Knowing what was unfolding in front of them.

The bearded man raised his shotgun and fired once into the air.

"Give 'em back to me!" he screamed again.

"What the fuck is going on," Trent exclaimed as he looked around. He looked up at the black church, surrounded by dead trees and plants, hemmed in by the iron fence. And straight in front of that division, the grass was alive. The plant life was verdant. Inside the confines of the church grounds, it seemed nothing was alive. And now this man was screaming for something to be given back... from *Sutter Cane?* If this was all an elaborate ruse. Actors playing a role, then it was an impressive feat of planning, but one Trent did not appreciate.

"Trent," Styles said sadly. "That man... The one shouting... Its Elijah Kirby."

Then it began.

The sound.

A deep groaning, as if the stones the building had been made of were now moving against themselves. A sound of a mechanism? Grinding, turning, scraping. It wasn't simply loud. It was a terrifying cacophony that made the small mob cower, grasping their ears. Making a few of them sob.

The sound though didn't hit Styles and Trent as bad. They both squinted in discomfort, but the pain was mainly on these men, as if the noise was a weapon aimed at them.

From behind Elijah, a weasel-thin man whimpered. "See what ya did? We gotta go, now! We can't beat him! I told you, we can't!"

Before he could answer, the church door began to slowly open with an uncomfortable creak that cut through the sounds of grinding stones.

No one could move. They could only stare.

The air around them changed, as a biting cold wind whipped up from nowhere, stirring the dust at their feet, and dragging leaves across the ground in spirals.

The church door creaked open bit by bit, until there, in the shadow of the doorway stood a small child.

A boy. Five years old. A mess of blond hair. Angelic. But looking drained and emotionless.

Elijah stepped forward, lowering his shotgun in disbelief, a relieved smile on his face.

"Johnny?" he called out with a trembling. "Johnny boy... come to daddy..."

Trent glared at Styles, annoyed he could not see the truth of what was happening. But he did know that she was hiding something. "What is this?" he barked. *"What do you know?"*

The wind around the church grew stronger and stronger, as the massive doors began to flap wildly, opening and slamming again in a violent rhythm, controlled by another force. The boy remained framed perfectly in the middle of the doorway, unmoving, as the wood crashed against the stone in a cacophonous beat. It was as if he was part of this show. Knew what was happening. And he stared at his father as if this were nothing more than an inconvenience.

"Johnny!" Elijah screamed again, as he started up the steps toward the doors, gripping his shotgun tighter to his chest.

He made it halfway up before the doors slammed and blew open once again, and in that millisecond instant, the boy was gone.

All that could be seen was the inside of the church, as if the boy simply vanished.

Slam.

Open.

Nothing.
Slam.
Open.
Nothing.
Slam.
Open.

Then there... where the boy had been, *he* stood.

Sutter Cane.

He stared out at Elijah, with a smile. It was nothing kind. It was a smile of malevolence. A smile of cruelty.

Trent's anger with Styles dropped as he stared at the man he had come here to find.

"Cane?" he said to himself. "Son of a bitch."

Before anyone could move, the church doors *slammed* shut again. The wood splintered, but this time, the door stayed shut. The crack echoed at them like a shockwave.

And from behind the church, a dozen black shapes careened into view.

Dogs. Jet-black. Large. Muscular. Dobermans with eyes like pits of cold tar. They raced in a perfect unison. One mind with many sharp fangs and a hunger.

The mob of men screamed.

They had no idea what to do. They were far out of their depths. Farmers acting like a militia.

Shotguns were fired as the dogs growled. The blasts were deafening. The aims were true.

Yet none of these dogs fell. None of the shots slowed them in the slightest.

Trent grabbed Styles and turned, running back toward the street, away from the violence that erupted in front of the church.

Not looking back, they could hear the screaming as they were attacked by the hounds. Flesh ripped. Blood spilled. Shots rang out.

But Trent and Styles didn't make it far.

As they turned toward the hotel, a small girl was standing, right in their path. She watched them with a wide, malicious smirk... one that curled over teeth that were far too large for her mouth. From her bulbous blue eyes, a thin trickle of blood trailed like tears down both cheeks.

Staggering to a stop, Trent stared at her, not knowing how to react.

"Who are you?" Styles said, the words coming out almost against her wishes. She did not want to interact with whatever this girl was, but found herself saying it, nevertheless.

The girl's head listed from side to side like a metronome. Her smirk not wavering.

"I'm the end," she said in a light, happy tone.

Without saying anything else, she turned and ran away, skipping lightly down the street to rejoin wherever the other children were.

Trent watched her leave, as a numbness filled him. A primal dread he had never felt before.

He'd now had enough. Whatever this was, whatever they'd stepped into, he wanted *out*. The job be damned. He was caught in the middle of something he didn't have patience for. If it was a ruse, he wanted to leave. If it was a book-made life, he wanted to leave. If it was the third ascension of Lord Oompah of the Eternal Marching Kazoo, or whatever made-up shit Cane wanted him to believe... he... wanted... to... leave.

Any eventuality or excuse would not change that fact.

But the town was not done with them yet.

Chapter Six

Trent packed his bag at a frantic pace, having only just put his clothes into the room's dresser less than an hour before. Now, he shoved his shirts, underwear, and socks unceremoniously back into his leather bag. No folding. Just urgency.

Across the room, Styles paced back and forth, her voice rising and falling in frustrated crescendos. She had not unpacked in her room next door, and her bag just sat on his bed.

"We can't leave," she repeated desperately for the third time. "Not now."

Trent didn't look up, he just kept on packing. "We've seen Cane. Job done. You're welcome."

"Yes!" she said. "*Exactly*. We've *seen* him."

"Good," Trent snapped. "That means I'm out. He's alive. Mystery solved. Your claim is void."

He slammed his bag shut, as if to punctuate his point.

"But the book—"

"Fuck the book," Trent said. "You want it? Go get it yourself. You walk right over to that lovely homely satanic fucking temple and ask him for it yourself. You obviously know way more about this than I do. Your policy is void. He's there."

Styles stepped closer to the bed. "Please Trent. The *book*—"

"Fuck the book. And *fuck you!*" He seethed. "I'm not helping anyone who's been lying to me since day one."

Her face fell. "What does that mean?"

"It means," he said, suddenly talking with a measured tone. Slowly and sternly. Each word filled with accusation. "You have known way more about this since I met you. I can tell a liar. I can tell when someone is holding stuff back. And you fit both of those categories. You plead ignorance, while your face says otherwise... Like... How about you tell me how you knew about that mob coming. You opened that curtain *knowing* the church was there without seeing it. You came into this town from the first moment as if you had been here many times and had known what was about to happen. I read the books too. There wasn't that much in there."

She glanced to the floor with a look of shame.

Trent laughed, bitter and short. "You can't bullshit

In The Mouth of Madness

a bullshitter, Styles. I know you've been fucking with me."

Still, no reply.

He pressed further, voice rising. "This whole goddamn thing is staged. You, Harglow, Cane, you're all in on it. You drop me in this carnival of creeps and expect me to run back to the National Enquirer, then sell them a story about a 'haunted town,' and boom, ten million more copies sold. I don't know how you got the place to just appear out of nowhere like that. Mirrors or some shit. And I'll be first to admit how damn impressive it's all been... but fuck me. You really think this would work? With *me*?"

"That's *not* what this is."

"Isn't it?" he said. "Because I think it is. And before I leave, I'm going to get someone in this two-bit set piece of a town to come clean. Then I'm gonna blow your little marketing stunt wide open, and Atlantic Insurance will probably take you to court and sue all of Sutter Cane profits right out of your bank."

Styles' voice broke as she shouted back. "You're wrong, Trent, so wrong!"

"Tell me... What the fuck are you hiding?"

She stared at him. Her lips parted, her breath shallow, eyes glassy. Quietly, she said, "Because you're... You're right."

Trent did not expect that reply. "What did you say?"

"Well, you're half right," she said softly. "This was

supposed to be a hoax. We did stage something. Harglow sent Cane away as a publicity stunt. To Florida. But he never showed up. We thought he'd just gone off-script and would call in. Three weeks ago, we realized... he'd vanished for real."

Trent raked his fingers through his hair, trying to piece it all together. "So, you came along to keep up appearances."

"I was sent with you to make it look good," she said. "Only..."

"Only we weren't supposed to find anything?"

"*Nothing* was supposed to be here. We had no idea about the cover art meaning anything."

He did not know what to say.

"And that's why I know what we're seeing is real. Because we didn't stage any of it. Not the boy on the road. Not the church. Not that little girl. Not Mrs. Pickman. None of it. It's all happening for real, and it's all in the book. That's how I knew about the men turning up... I even knew about the girl with blood in her eyes."

Trent stared at her for a long beat. "You're lying."

"I'm *not*."

"You seem to forget I read Cane's books too. There's nothing about mobs or little girls."

"Not in the published ones, Trent. But in the new one... *In the Mouth of Madness*. We got the first chapters, remember? And he described all of it. The mob. The boy in the church. The girl. Even Cane himself being there. He even pitched the rest of the story to me. I didn't really understand what he was saying. Said that *he* would be a main character in it."

"What about his agent," Trent said, suddenly remembering that axe-wielding madman and that this was more than just a parlor trick. That some people actually died. "Did *he* read it too, what was he in all this?"

"I don't know... It was all in fragments. Whole sections missed out. Just to show us what some flavors of what he wrote. But I do know, the new book... it's about the end. The end of everything. It all begins here. In this place, and it starts with the corruption of the children."

Trent shook his head. "How do I know you haven't just hired a bunch of actors to play out Cane's lunatic fantasy?"

"You don't," she said. "But I *know* it's all real. I read it. Now it's here. Just like in the pages. Everything... Everything is in it."

"No! It's fiction. Fiction, Styles! There are no monsters. No old Gods!"

She suddenly thought of something. "You want to believe me? You've got to check the paintings in the lobby again. You'll see. It'll be just like in the new book."

"And what will I see?"

"You'll see that we can't escape this. This is it. This is Cane's world."

. . .

Trent walked down the stairs like a man heading into a war he didn't believe in... slow, deliberate, already defeated. Why he wasn't in the car by now, leaving this madness behind, he didn't know. Maybe part of him needed to see how deep the rabbit hole really went.

The lobby sat in silence and the reception desk was empty. It smelled the same. Seemed the same. Looking around he paused, reached into his jacket, pulled out a cigarette, and lit it with a tremble in his hands.

This shouldn't be getting to him. It was all so ludicrous.

He turned to face the paintings, just as Styles told him to do.

Three canvases. Each one was innocent in content as he first saw them, but—

Wait.

He looked closer. They were not as he remembered at all. Sure, in one the cows were still in the sunlit field. But now they were not placid and dumb animals grazing. Now, their eyes were leaking red streaks. One had a mouth full of sharp, human-like teeth, bared mid-chew as red spilled out over its chin.

In the second, a boy played fetch with a dog. But the boy's joy was no longer there. He now looked terrified. The dog had become twisted, impossibly so. With extra legs, muzzle elongated, eyes hollowed out... the same thing he saw the children chasing in the street.

The third showed two lovers by a creek. They were the same couple, in the same clothes, in the same pose... but their heads had turned. Their eyes now stared out at Trent; they too were hollow like the dog's. And there was something else in the distance, rising behind them, emerging from the very end of the creek. A shape, undefined.

The colors in the images were also richer now, the brushstrokes appearing deeper, giving more of a texture. They were less impressionistic and more realistic. Like Cane's cover art. They didn't just seem more real, but they looked more *alive*.

Trent, though, was not freaked out. He saw it as yet another trick. A swap of the canvasses.

Cute, he thought. *But not that cute.*

A voice rang out, from behind him. "No smoking, please..."

He turned, slightly startled.

Mrs. Pickman stood there behind the desk, smiling her usual grandmotherly smile, but her eyes were different now. Puffy. Red-veined. And she stared at him without a single blink.

"Apologies." Trent held up his cigarette, as he took a step closer.

"It bothers my husband," she explained.

"Not a problem. I was just leaving," he smiled, examining her expression. Was it fear? No... more like a restrained anger? "I just stopped to admire your art."

"Beauties, aren't they?" she said, suddenly offering a twitching smile.

"Sure are. Ms. Styles said you painted them yourself?"

Mrs. Pickman frowned. "Ms. Styles? Who?"

"The woman I checked in with. Have you known each other long?"

"Oh. The pretty young thing.... No, I don't know her at all. Does she know me?"

Well-acted, Trent mused. He continued to try to trip her up. "So... you didn't paint them?"

Mrs. Pickman laughed, but her mouth still twitched slightly, as if a tremor was running through her body. "Hell no, not little ol' me."

"Well, you've got a great place here." He paused for a second. "Uh... Mrs. Pickman, may I ask... Are you okay? You look quite tired."

Her twitchy smile didn't change. "Not sleeping much."

"Me too," he said, still studying her. "Just taking a walk to wake me up a bit."

She leaned forward to the desk, just a little, then smiled even wider.

"Good idea," she said. "You go do that."

Behind the desk, at her feet, something scratched against the wood.

Noticing it, Trent smiled as he tried to peer over the countertop.

But Mrs. Pickman moved to block him, still with

her intense and off-putting smile. "Goodbye then," she said. "Have a nice walk."

He realized she wasn't the easy nut to crack that he'd assumed she was. So, with a small nod and a shrug of his mouth, he turned and walked out, not wanting to waste any more time.

As the door shut, the lobby fell back into silence.

Until another scratch sounded from behind the desk, coupled with it, a low groan.

With a sneer, Mrs. Pickman glanced down at her feet.

"Oh, hush now," she moaned.

There on the floor, a withered old man lay naked. Mr. Pickman. The skin over his skeletal body was a patchwork of bruises and cuts. One of his wrists had been handcuffed with a long chain to his wife's ankle.

He pawed at her leg with long, yellowed fingernails. Not in anger but begging. A useless attempt at getting some pity.

Mrs. Pickman looked down at him without emotion, then swung her boot hard into his face.

Bedroom number ten was washed in the murky light of dusk, as Styles sat on the edge of her bed, the telephone receiver pressed to her ear. All she could hear was the cold tone of white noise. No dial tone, no click, no signal. Just that endless, whispering fuzzy sound that made her skin itch.

She hung up slowly. With a slow breath, she furrowed her brow and turned her gaze to the copy of *The Hobb's End Horror* on the nightstand.

What was it Cane had told her whilst pitching his new book? That it was a story about the end of all things?

No. I said it <u>was</u> the end of all things.

The wind rolled coldly down the main street as Trent paced down the middle of it. He had left the hotel an hour ago, and had walked around this small town, street after street, looking for anything, *anyone*, but found only desolation. No people at all.

With his collar up and another cigarette dying slowly between his lips. The sun had now dropped, and the street lamps, what few of them still worked, had started to bathe the concrete in yellowing light.

He hadn't meant to walk for this long. Hadn't meant to stay out. But Styles' voice was still rattling around in his skull like a pinball. The paintings. The details of the new book.

All the bullshit that was being forced on him to believe.

For what?

Still... his steps hadn't taken him toward the car. They'd taken him around and around Hobb's End.

In The Mouth of Madness

He had almost given up hope but had seen the light through the glass.

A flicker of neon. Red and stuttering.

The Crooked Star. A bar he could have sworn was boarded up when he walked past earlier.

As he walked in, a jukebox hummed in the corner, its warped speakers leaking out some slow, dying country song. Every note sounded tired and crackled, like it had been played a thousand times.

The whole place reeked of cigarettes, whiskey and mildew, and didn't look like it had seen sunlight in years.

There were people here, unlike the rest of town. They were sat in booths and at the bar. Weathered men with broken fingernails and half-finished drinks. No women. No children. They didn't even look up when he entered. Nobody smiled. Nobody asked where he was from. They just drank, quiet and isolated, like each sip had kept something worse at bay. He didn't recognize any of them, but they all looked like they were laborers or farmers.

Trent moved to the bar and took a seat, easing himself onto the vinyl stool, not trusting that it would not immediately collapse under his weight.

"Be with you in a bit," the barman grumbled.

Trent pulled the notebook from his coat pocket and flipped it open.

He scrawled a few things. Words. Clues. Accusations.

- *Hobb's End – staged? A set?*
- *People – paid off for sure*
- *Paintings – rigged/planned*
- *Harglow/Styles/Cane –* BULLSHITTERS!!!

He tapped the pen against the paper. It was all too clean, he thought. Too rehearsed. Every person he'd seen, every building, every event, it was like they'd been choreographed. Designed to press all the right buttons just when he arrived to witness it. A masquerade being performed just for him... He scrawled in his notebook again:

- *Endgame – More sales?*

Maybe Cane's sales were all bluster. Maybe Arcane just told everyone how big and famous Cane was, and we just believed it? The bookstore riots would have all been set up as well. Did Arcane really spend all this money to make a few more books sell?

"You a writer?" a voice rasped beside him.

Trent looked up.

The man beside him was familiar. It was the bearded man from outside the church. Elijah Kirby. Now he was slumped over the bar and looked beaten down. One of his hands had been wrapped in a dirty shred of fabric, a makeshift bandage. The other nursed a cheap glass of brown liquor. On his pale and sweaty face were lines of bloody scratches. He had lost the fight with the dogs but managed to survive.

The dog attack had looked very real, as did these wounds, Trent thought. Maybe that scene went off book and got out of hand?

"Am I a writer?" he replied. "Nah, I'm a detective of sorts... from Brooklyn."

Elijah snorted. "Brooklyn, huh? Then you should take a hint, mister. *Leave.* This ain't no town for tourists."

Trent looked around the room. He only now realized that most of the men here were the same ones from the church. They too were bloodied and battered, pale and sickly looking.

Maybe I can convince these guys? Trent thought. *Maybe they'll want to tell me the truth after being hurt?*

"You mind me asking... How much is Cane paying you?" he asked under his breath. "I won't tell anyone, I promise."

Elijah didn't answer his question. "Sutter Cane's nothing but a dead man," he said, grimacing. "Been one since he started messin' in that church. Now something's leaking out. Took the little ones first, it did. He read his book to 'em, you see? They brought it home from school... It took some fast. Some slow. But it took 'em all in the end."

His eyes gleamed with an honest look of fear.

"You hear things. You see things. You can't stop 'em. It gets in your blood. In your sleep. It's in your skin." There was no sarcasm in his words. Only warning. "Don't let it get to you. Don't look at it. Just... Just *get out.*"

Trent looked amused, as he pulled out his pack of cigarettes from his jacket and lit one. He did not speak until after he took a long drag and exhaled very slowly.

"You guys are good, I gotta say I'm damn impressed," he said. "You, the woman at the hotel... really, really good. If there were awards of insurance fraud, I'd vote for all of you."

Styles could feel it. The pull. Something telling her to leave the room, leave the hotel and walk up the street toward the church.

And that is what she was doing.

Step after step, she walked slowly. Past the shattered windshields of abandoned cars. Past the boarded-up shops. It was only now that she noticed that the whole street was somehow littered with spent ammunition shells. Bullet casings spread like breadcrumbs. She stepped over them carefully wondering what kind of war had happened here.

She did not know why she did, but she was headed toward the church.

Something moved just a few feet ahead; a small red ball rolled out of the shadows of an alleyway and stopped at her feet.

A child stepped out from the darkness. A boy, no

In The Mouth of Madness

older than six. Dressed in shorts and a T-shirt with no shoes on. He was filthy from head to toe.

Crouching, Styles picked up the ball.

He moved like a broken puppet, his limbs looked too long, his skin was too taut. and too pale. And just like the girl from earlier, his eyes were bulbous, bloodied and he had a grin full of teeth that were too large for his mouth.

"Give it back," he said. His voice little more than a gurgle.

She handed it out to him slowly, wondering what had happened to him. "Where do you live?" she asked.

"With *you*," the boy grinned wider.

Styles frowned. "No. I mean who takes care of you?"

"*You* do."

And with that, he suddenly turned and ran, if it could be called running. His limbs didn't move like a child. He twitched forward as if he were being yanked and stumbled and staggered away at speed.

Styles stood back up, realizing she should have stayed inside.

Then came a whimper from behind her.

She slowly turned and came face to face with the little girl, but she wasn't alone.

More children stood quietly around her. Smiling the same oversized smile as the girl. Their clothes were spattered in blood and were all as filthy as the boy.

Sat next to them was the dog-like creature they had

been chasing. Styles could see it was somewhat canine, but it had two more legs than it should. With sweaty, clammy pock-marked skin its fur was non-existent. Its empty sockets somehow still stared up at her...

And as she stared at it, terrified and frozen, she remembered Cane's description of this creature; *'a mongrel built from the scraps of forgotten nightmares stitched by a god with palsied hands and no love for symmetry.'*

The little girl smiled. Her teeth had now changed. They were still too large for her mouth but were now sharper. Pointier. More predatory.

"You're our mommy," she said with a laugh, the words muffled behind her toothy maw. "And do you know what today is?" she asked.

The other children began to laugh too. As did the same little boy who had run in the opposite direction, and somehow, now was there among the others, joining in the giggling fang-filled chorus.

The girl's eyes were almost completely round as they glared at Styles hungrily. "Give up?" she asked in a whisper. "Today is mommy's day."

With a gasp, Styles could not face them anymore. She turned and ran in the only direction she could... Straight toward the black church.

Trent cursed under his breath as he searched Styles' room, checking the bathroom, behind the curtains, even under the bed. There was nothing. No sign of her. Her coat was still draped over the chair, and the air still smelled like her perfume, but she was gone.

He slammed the bathroom door shut behind him. "Shit," he grimaced. "Just what I need."

He grabbed the phone from the nightstand and put it up to his ear.

Before he could dial any number, he heard it.

The white noise. No dial tone.

He quickly hung it up, resisting the urge to throw it across the room. He could not help the sad laugh that escaped his lips.

"Of course," he sighed.

Sitting on the end of the bed, he wondered how long he should wait for Styles, if at all.

He glanced toward the door, then around the room.

The Hobb's End Horror sat on the sheets next to him. With another sigh, he picked it up and reluctantly started to read.

Styles walked through the iron gate, past the dead grass, and up the steps to the entrance of the church.

The wood of the doors was dark and old, still with the long cracks covering them from earlier, when they slammed shut.

Getting closer she noticed something on one of them. An inscription had been etched into the panel.

Carefully, she ran her fingers over the letters as she read aloud: "Let these doors be sealed..."

"...By our Lord God," Trent whispered, reading from the book as he sat on the edge of the bed, "in His year 1788... and let any who dare enter this unholy site be damned forever."

The world outside the black church felt like another existence entirely, as Styles pushed open the door and walked in, letting it shut behind her.

Lit only by the dull moonlight coming in through the stained-glass windows, she moved down the nave, her boots echoing off the large stone tiles.

She walked by the many rows of decaying pews, rotting and crumbling where they sat.

She had not been in here before, but she knew to go to the staircase at the back. The staircase that led to the largest steeple tower.

She had thought about calling out, to see if Cane was around, but her nerves got the better of her. She felt like the very church itself was watching her, listening.

Ahead, just as she thought, a narrow staircase spiraled up behind the altar like a spine to the whole building.

She hesitated only for a second, before placing her hand on the cold banister.

She started to climb.

Each metal step creaked, and she remembered Cane's words once more. *'The steeple was not just a tower. It was the throat. And what lay above it was the mouth. We were never meant to climb toward it or go through that door. But like a blind mouse, we could always be counted on to do what we should not dare to do.'*

And despite this, she carried on, barely able to steady her breath.

The attic room sat at the top of the steeple.

In front of the closed door, Styles collected all her nerves. Forced her doubt down and reached out for the handle.

From somewhere on the other side, a sound soon started, causing her to pause. Soft at first, the rapid *click-click-click*. The sound of keys on a typewriter. Familiar. Rhythmic. Surreal. But the sound started to grow louder, angrier. Each key struck, sounded like a pounding.

Louder.

Louder.

Heavier.

VIOLENT.

CLICK, CLICK, CLICK, CLICK.

And then... sudden silence.

She turned.

This was getting too much.

She was about to leave...

...That's when something unseen seized her.

She didn't scream, she didn't get the chance. A colossal force yanked her upward, as the door flung open on its own accord. She was dragged into the darkness on the other side.

As she crossed the threshold, the door slammed behind her with a thunderous *bang*.

The attic should have been no larger than a closet. A narrow space, used for storage. But now, somehow, it was a vast, cathedral-like room. One that seemed to violate the laws of reality.

The surrounding walls were swallowed in shadow, and the reflective marble floor stretched further ahead than should be possible.

In the middle of this space, in a lonely beam of light cast down from no visible source, sat a simple wooden table. Upon it rested an old typewriter.

Behind it... Sutter Cane.

He didn't rise when Styles had been dragged in and thrown to the floor.

He didn't even flinch.

He just kept typing.

Styles groaned as she slowly got to her feet.

In The Mouth of Madness

Whatever had forced her in, had now let her go. She looked around nervously.

"Linda..." Cane said without looking up. His voice was beyond calm, it was friendly. "It is so lovely to see you again, not that it is a surprise."

His fingers never stopped moving as he spoke. Never even slowed.

"I'm sure you are aware, but I am afraid I do not need you to edit this book anymore. But you can witness it from the inside looking out."

She stepped unsteadily forward but was unable to stop herself.

"Sutter?" her voice said nervously.

Still, he typed.

"I started with the children, Linda" he said. "Because they're quick learners. Then they took it to their parents. And the parents... oh, they spread it amongst themselves like it was the bubonic plague. Now they're all becoming. And they are watching the flames burn higher and higher."

Styles kept inching closer, moving forward in step with the rhythm of the typing.

"Becoming what?" she asked, dreading whatever answer he may offer.

The typing suddenly stopped as Cane looked up at her.

"What? They will become what I've already become."

Sutter Cane

She was close enough to see the sweat on his brow, the ink stains on his fingers... and the impossible.

He rose from his chair and seemed like a man now revealed itself as something far worse. As he turned, where his back should have been, there was another person. Another torso. Another face. His body was two halves of a whole, each side facing a different way, each from a different reality. The side that typed, that smiled at her was human. Was the Sutter Cane she knew. The other... The other was... *not*.

Styles gasped as she saw its face, monstrous, contorted, eyeless, grinning at her.

As this other side of Cane spoke, its voice sounded similar but distorted.

"I became.... One of *them*."

He raised a hand and motioned to the darkness around him. As he did, a cacophony of shrieking, horrifying howls erupted from the shadows. A choir of grotesque, unseen things.

As these cries sounded, a wind suddenly whipped through this attic like a hurricane had torn through the very fabric of space and time.

Styles turned to look, as the shadows behind Cane began to undulate, and a deeper darkness burst out from within. A black so deep it drained her emotion just to witness it.

As the darkness grew, and the wind gusted against her with a terrible force, she opened her mouth to scream... But no sound came out.

Then, it vanished.

Then, the wind died.

Then Styles' legs gave way.

The other side of Cane lunged forward and grabbed her, pulling her close to him.

"The secret of my success," he whispered, in garbled words. "All those stories of horrible, slimy things trying to get back into the world... They are all true. All of them. I had no idea. And what I saw... was beautiful."

He carefully dragged her toward the table and placed her down into his chair.

"I'm letting them in, Linda," he said. "They gave me the power to make my stories breathe. And now, I'm writing *our world* into *theirs*."

He moved her face in front of the stacked pile of manuscript pages.

"And here is the instrument of their homecoming. What you are looking for. The new bible. Fiction becomes reality... and reality becomes a memory. I just haven't written the ending yet."

His hands grabbed her face, forcing her to close the pages.

"Read it, Linda. *Read it and learn the true nature of your existence.*"

As she was forced closer, as the fear took over her, she could not help opening her eyes. The letters upon the paper swam across in a pool of words. A terrifying, eternal pool.

Throughout the large room, Styles' scream filled each corner.

"I can see!" she cried out. "*I can see!*"

And the blood came. It burst in spiderweb patterns from the whites of her eyes as the vessels ruptured. She shook, unable to look away. Her scream was not a scream, it was a revelation.

"I *CAN SEEEEEEEEEEE!*"

From the outside, the steeple rose into the night sky. Barely visible against the storm clouds that had arrived.

And from within the top of the tower, deep in another reality, Styles' screams echoed across Hobb's End.

Chapter Seven

Trent jolted awake to the knocking on his hotel door. Not loud. Not frantic. Just steady and deliberate.

His mind was slow to catch up as he rubbed his eyes. The room was dark, save for the moonlight through the open curtains.

He sat up, still dressed, then moved toward the door in a sluggish daze. He was exhausted. There was too much weirdness crammed into one week.

He should have driven home. Just got in the car and left Styles to her own devices. She was part of this, and there was no reason he should feel any sympathy for her. How could he trust anything she said anymore?

When he opened the door, she collapsed into him.

Styles.

She was soaking with not just sweat, but also

blood. Soaking through her sleeves, her blouse, covering her hands, matting her hair and dripping down her face.

Her breathing was weak and gasping. She had no words and was a dead weight in his arms.

"Styles?" he said, stunned by the suddenness of the situation. "*Styles!*"

He carried her to the bed and laid her down, not caring that the blood was now staining the bedsheets below.

Her eyes were open but empty, staring into nothing, she seemed catatonic.

Trent rushed quickly to the bathroom, soaked a washcloth in cold water, then returned looking worried. He quickly wiped at the blood on her face, her neck. It all smeared away easily enough.

The more he wiped away, the more he saw that her skin had no cuts, no wounds, no visible injury of any kind. This blood was not hers.

"Where did the blood come from?" he whispered to himself before repeating it louder to her. "Styles? Where the hell did the blood come from?"

That's when her eyes focused, and she looked directly at him.

She lunged, grabbing at his arms as if she were trying to claw her way back. Her breathing was as rapid as her speeding pulse.

He tried to calm her, pulling her closer. "What happened? What did you do?"

In The Mouth of Madness

"I'm losing me," she said, her voice fractured. Barely able to keep hold of the words through her breath. "I'm losing me, John... help me... please. I'm not holding together. *I'm losing me!*"

"Was it Harglow?" he asked.

But she was not able to listen. She was trapped in her terror. "I *saw* the book," she said with a sudden crazed smile. "Don't read it, John. Don't even look at it. He's opened the door. It's already started. I looked... I looked... and now I'm not me anymore. I'm losing *me*. You have to tell me I exist. You have to *say it!* Tell me I'm *real!*"

"You're real," he whispered. "You're *right* here. You're safe now. You're with me."

She pulled back and screamed again.

"I'm losing me, John! Don't read it! Please!"

Trent eased her back down, hands on her shoulders, trying to pin her panic back into her body.

"Stay here," he said. "Don't move. I'm just going to find a phone that works. Something. Anything."

He quickly turned and rushed out of the room.

He moved fast, past faded wallpaper and flickering bulbs, as he raced down the stairs, down into the lobby.

The desk was empty.

He hurried over and hit the bell with the flat of his palm, once, twice.

"Come on, you old bitch," he muttered.

But no one came.

He rang the bell again.

"Hello? Mrs. Pickman?" he called out.

Nothing.

Looking around the desk, there was no phone on the counter. His attention then moved to the office.

Like most places he went, the smell was the first thing he noticed, always had been. He always had a keen sense of smell, and for a New Yorker that was not always a good thing. But here, it was not like the lobby. Not musty, but instead reeked of spoiled meat. Metallic and rotten.

He looked around for a phone, but there was none. It was not an office, it was just an empty room. No chair, no table, no files, nothing. Just an open doorway ahead leading to a set of stairs going down.

A sound ahead caught his attention.

A dull, repetitive whack coming from below.

A crunching sound.

He needed to help Styles. He needed to find a phone... But that sound... *That sound...*

He knew where the steps went. *The Hobb's End Horror* told him as much.

Trent could not stop himself from walking down, following the thwacking sounds.

The further he went, the louder and more disturbing the sounds became.

Louder.

Wetter.

When he got to the bottom, in the darkened basement, his hand found the light switch along the wall by

In The Mouth of Madness

the last step. Without hesitation, he flicked it on... and immediately wished he hadn't.

The bulb was at the far end of the room. When it snapped to life, it bathed everything in an orange glow and cast a huge shadow across the room.

A large shape was in front of it, silhouetted by the light, blocking it out with its huge form.

It was her.

Mrs. Pickman.

Or at least the top half was. Her face caught the light as she turned, but she was not looking at Trent nor paying him any attention, she was glaring at what was on the floor in front of her.

She was there, obscenely malformed. There were no legs. No hips. No bones that moved the way bones should. Instead, something else was holding her up, something living. A mass of shifting flesh that rippled and slithered, brushing the floor and the walls as it moved. It never stopped moving. A dozen slick shapes slid over each other, too fast to focus on. *Tentacles.*

In her hands, she held a fire axe.

The sound he had heard coming down had come from the axe's impact, over and over, landing on what was broken in front of her, still writhing on the floor.

The second shape still manacled to her with handcuffs.

Mr. Pickman.

He was barely alive. His frail body covered in gaping, bleeding wounds where the axe had already broken in. Flesh torn, bone snapped. One hand stretched out toward Trent, pleading in silence.

The axe came down once more and took his hand with it.

No screams came from him, just instinctive cowering, trying to move away from the assault his wife now wrought upon him.

Trent's voice was weak with shock, but for some reason, he forced a strangled whisper. "Mrs. Pickman...?" He said her name out of surprise, as he tried to understand the sight in front of him, but he could not. He remembered it from the book, but seeing it now, and smelling it. His head told him it was all fake, but his gut told him something completely different.

She turned toward him, and her form came more into view. Her face was almost human. *Almost.* Slightly too long, too stretched. Eyes too wide. A grin that carried too many sharp teeth.

"You want some too, buddy?" she asked, her voice disturbingly sweet and happy.

Trent stumbled back, hitting the bottom step and falling back onto the stairs. He did not know what to do... He could not listen to his gut... He could not face this being real.

"You're acting," he gasped, not believing what he was seeing. "None of this is real!"

She slithered toward him, the axe dripping with blood, the tentacles flicking around her.

In The Mouth of Madness

"I'm hungry," she cried out.

As the tentacles approached, his gut reaction took control. He scrambled up the stairs, two steps at a time and didn't stop until he was back in the lobby, racing toward his room.

He didn't notice the paintings.

He just ran on by.

They were different again.

The pastoral scenes had been replaced with abominations.

The cows that had once grazed in a field were now a thrashing horde of tentacled monstrosities, clawing up chunks of earth to expose human corpses buried beneath.

The boy who had once played with his dog had changed. Now he was eating the dog, raw, grinning, blood down his chin.

The lovers in the third painting were no longer embracing. They were fusing, merging into something neither human nor creature, locked in an impossible three-way embrace with the twisted, crawling thing that had emerged from the creek behind.

None of these looked like paintings anymore.

They looked like photographs.

And each thing that was in the paintings was now looking out. Looking out at Trent as he ran up the stairs. Turning as he rushed by.

. . .

Trent burst into room number nine. Panic coursed through his veins and confusion was consuming him. He had not time to dwell on what he had seen...He had to go... but his mind still spun. *An act. It's all an act. Special effects. Latex puppets... It has to be. It has to be. A huge, elaborate haunted house. Please let it be a haunted house.*

Haunting implies death, John Trent. This is all very much alive.

Styles was not on the bed. The room was empty. But it wasn't the same as when he'd left it.

The walls had been savaged.

Deep gouges scored the plaster, large claw-like marks that stretched from carpet to ceiling.

He could not understand what had happened.

"Styles?" he called, but there was no answer.

He noticed the bathroom door was closed.

Still in shock, Trent had trouble thinking straight. He hurried over to the bathroom door and pounded his hand on it.

"Styles? Are you in there?" he called out, his voice teetering on the edge. "We need to go. We need to go, *now!*"

From inside, her voice could be heard. It sounded

strange. Not sleepy, not scared. Just... distant and resigned.

"Too late... John. It is too late."

He pounded on the door again. "Come on! We have to leave, right now!"

A sound answered him, not any words, but a playful giggle. An unhinged lilting laugh that sounded like she was masking tears beneath mania.

Looking down, Trent stepped back as he noticed a liquid seeping out from under the bathroom door. Thick, dark water, like crimson-colored oil, carrying with it a stench of rancid waste. In its slow movement, it brought with it... things. Small, pale, translucent, twitching forms that writhed like worms.

"Styles, please..." he said, stepping away from the liquid.

He looked around the room, hoping to find anything he could use to break the door down. But there was nothing here. Nothing except *The Hobb's End Horror* that sat on the sideboard, looking up at him, as if mocking him with its very presence.

Exasperated, he glanced out of the window.

There, on the other side of the street, moving along the sidewalk, was the strange dog-like creature. Moving in a stilted, unnatural gait on its six fleshy legs, as it passed beneath the flickering glow of the street lamp.

Then the sounds came.

The sounds of the town screaming.

Not with one voice, but dozens. All crying out in agony. From every house and building.

Moving toward the window, Trent opened it, trying to hear what was happening. As he did, the collection of screams became cacophonous. And with them came sounds of smashing and crashing. Sounds of chaos and destruction building up from every direction.

Trent was a brave man. At least he hoped he was. Yet hearing this, changed that concept. He had to go. Go now. And to hell with Styles. She had to be part of this. He wanted to believe her, and earlier she seemed genuinely scared, and affected. But there was no way.

He was about to turn around, as the bathroom door unlocked with a *click*.

As the door creaked open, Trent could not bring himself to turn and look. He stood facing the window and closed his eyes. Every muscle in his body locked into place as he heard footsteps squelch out onto the carpet, the now wet and oily carpet. Her feet squished until she came up behind him.

"Styles... Linda?" he said. Trying to keep his composure. "You got me good, okay? I fell for it. I'll sign off on whatever you want. Get you that payout. You deserve it... Let's just go..."

Her reply came through quivering lips, broken up by sobs. She struggled to form the words.

"We *are* home..." she answered.

He turned. He didn't want to, but he had to.

What he saw pulled the breath from his lungs and sent him stumbling backward, into the window, cracking as he hit against it.

Her face. Half looked as it always had, flushed and scared, yet still Linda Styles. Still the beautiful Linda Styles. But the other half...

That other half of her face was warped and twisted. Her skin drooped and sagged from her distended skull like it was raw meat, like it half-melted and reattached in the wrong places. Her eye had rolled back into its socket, showing only the white.

A single tear ran down her normal cheek, while from the monstrous side, a bead of blood traced a slow path toward her jutting chin.

As she spoke, she sounded as if her voice were in another room.

"I lost me..." she cried in a tortured tone.

Trent wanted to bolt to the side, to run around her, but she grabbed him first.

With a sudden motion, she smacked him aside, sending him sprawling across the bed.

"Read the book, John," she said. Her voice sharper now, more present. Without any trace of hurt or fear. "It's easier when you *know*. You need to *know*."

She came at him again and grabbed him by the throat.

This was not fake. He felt the pain of her relentless grip.

Sutter Cane

He didn't register the door shattering behind him as he was hurled out of the room and into the hallway.

He was airborne for half a second before his body collided with the wall, the impact crushing the plastered wall inwards. Bits of wood and debris cracked out around him as he slumped to the floor in a bruised pile.

From inside the room, she was still coming after him.

Trent had to move.

He didn't want to know what she would do to him next.

Scrambling toward the staircase. He could hear Styles screaming after him in a fury, as he bounded down. He didn't look back, not even once.

Bursting through the front doors of the hotel, Trent was out in the street before he even realized it.

It should have been quiet, at midnight in a small New England town. But it wasn't. He had forgotten the noises he heard from the window. But here now, he had run into a chaos of inhuman noises and sounds of destruction. An orchestra of madness.

He turned, slowly, scared.

The streets were empty, but things in every building, every window, every closed door around him could be heard. Noises coming from inside each of them. Voices in each structure. Shouting. Laughing. Screaming. Crying.

In The Mouth of Madness

All at once. Some sounded like children. Others like animals. But most didn't sound like either. They sounded like things far from human, mimicking humanity.

Within those noises, he could hear snaps and cracks. Moist, awful noises.

He had to get to the car. In the madness of the moment, he had trouble thinking. The noises grew and grew. With each snap, each crash, each pained scream, each horrible laugh they got louder. Sicker.

Throwing his hands over his ears, Trent ran. Not to his car, as that was further down the street, but to the last place he saw people. People who did not seem to want to be a part of this. He crossed over to The Crooked Star.

The door slammed behind him. Muffling the screams outside behind the glass and wood.

Trent leaned against it, panting, his chest heaving. He did not remember the last time he had run. Maybe not since he was a child. But the years of smoking were now felt in his lungs as he struggled to breathe, wheezing.

Outside, the town had become a feral din. But in the pub, it was silence. A cold and hollow silence.

He straightened slowly, ignoring the sweat that dripped down his face.

The place was empty.

Walking in, he needed this to be over. Whatever game these lunatics were playing.

John Trent, lunacy is a word that the fearful devised.
 A word to brand, to lock away when they feared.
 A label for that which doesn't fit neatly into a small, soft world of light switches and traffic signs.
 They say lunacy as if it were a condition, a disease you can catch.
 But what if it's the cure?
 What if the real sickness is needing the world to make sense?

Trent was mentally grasping at straws. Not wanting to hear the dissenting voices in his head. To him, it seemed real, felt real, but he could not see how. A twisted piece of performance art or a psychological experiment?

Drugs... Maybe he had been drugged?

Look around you, John Trent, you were not drugged.

He *was* John Trent. He knew the angles. He had made a career out of seeing through scams. No matter how elaborate or nonsensical. This was a trick. It *had* to be.

In The Mouth of Madness

He looked around and saw the bar, or what was left of it.

It looked like the place had been ransacked. Barstools had been overturned and broken; shattered bottles bled into sticky puddles across cracked floorboards. It was a far cry from the place he had sat in only a short time ago.

Walking further in, he noticed that the walls were gouged just like in his bedroom, with dozens of slashes and scratches covering each side.

"You still here?" a voice asked with a spluttering, pained cough. A tired and broken voice from the far end of the bar, hidden in the shadows by the jukebox.

Trent turned, nearly slipping on a pool of beer beneath his shoes.

The figure was slumped, back against the wall. A shotgun rested across his lap, gripped by both hands.

It was Elijah Kirby. Except now he appeared like a man weeks into a siege. Hair wild and matted, beard thick with dried blood. His shirt was torn into ribbons, the flesh beneath it blackened with bruises and cuts that stood open. One entire cheek on his face was missing... not cut but *torn* away. The hole gaped with raw, exposed sinew. Some of his molars gleamed wetly through the ruined meat around it.

"Busy night?" Elijah asked with a sad smile. "I told you to leave... You should have listened to me."

Trent laughed, high-pitched and shrill, not because it was funny, but because it was the only defense he had left. His hand shook as he fumbled with a lighter, trying to light a cigarette from his pocket. The flame danced around the tip. Flickering. Refusing him.

With a grunt, he lowered the lighter again and glared at the man. "It's all special effects," he snapped. "Hidden speakers. Animatronics." He shook his head as he tried to gather his thoughts. "The budget must be enormous."

Trent tried the lighter again and failed. The sparks came, but no flame. Exasperated he threw it to the floor and let the cigarette drop from his lips.

"You ever think," Elijah said calmly, not reacting, "that maybe you're not foolin' anyone but yourself?"

Trent's mask cracked, just for a second. His face twitched. He growled and pointed a finger at the man. Losing all his composure.

"You're *actors*. You're not real. This is a *set*. Some elaborate, viral campaign. The oldest trick in the book, mess with the insurance guy, make it seem like the author's gone crazy and vanished into his own story. Genius, but fucking demented!"

Elijah thought for a second and moaned as he spoke. "The only thing I can't remember..." he pondered slowly, "...is what came first. Us... or the books."

Trent was unable to hold back his anger. Raw, furious denial that came in waves. Grabbing a glass from the bar, he hurled it at the man. Not aimed at him, but above. The only thing he could do.

It exploded against the wall above the jukebox. Elijah didn't flinch. Didn't move. Just watched as the glass fell around him.

"We are *not* in a Sutter Cane story!" Trent bellowed. "You people are *phonies*! Or psychos! Or both! This isn't real! *This is not real!*"

Elijah started laughing with a glassy-eyed grin.

"Reality's not what it used to be," he said in amusement.

Trent staggered against the bar, his balance faltering. "God, this place makes my head hurt," he muttered, clutching his temple.

"Hey..." Elijah said gently.

Trent turned away. He didn't want to hear more of the lies.

"No, really. C'mere. You oughta see this. If you wanna know what's *really* going on. I'll let you in on the secret."

Trent glanced back, compelled despite himself.

The man tapped the jagged edge of his wound with the tip of his shotgun barrel.

"See this?" he said. "This was done by a five-year-old. *My* five-year-old. She did me right after she did it to her mom."

Elijah's pupils begun to swell, as they starting to glow a sickly blue. His skin started to pulse. Stretch, as something began to slither beneath it.

Trent didn't speak. He just stood aghast.

"You're *alone*," Elijah whispered.

A sound. A grotesque *ripping* from behind Elijah. From out of his back.

Two thick tentacles burst from this spine with loud snapping of bones and ripping of skin. Veined and glistening, they raised up and slapped against the floorboards in front of him, twitching and writhing. One of them struck a beer bottle, sending it smashing to the floor.

The man's body was changing. Bones shifting their form. Skin pulling to tearing. His back hunched backwards. His jaw unhinged and lolled loose from his skull.

He was not dead though. He was still very much alive.

He started at Trent with something close to apology, as he picked up the shotgun and pointed it at his own face.

"Don't," Trent whimpered. Unable to fathom what was happening.

"I have to," Elijah replied. "He wrote me this way."

The trigger clicked and in a thunderclap of flame and red mist, the shotgun blasted through Elijah's head. His skull broke open toward Trent like a flower.

But the tentacles... they weren't dead, and they were not done. Tearing themselves from Elijah's slumped body, they slithered away into the shadows. One vanished beneath the bar. The other crawled into the jukebox beside them, sparking a brief flicker of static across its shattered glass.

Trent stared.

Unable to breathe.

Unable to blink.

Something had shifted.

This wasn't a prank. This wasn't a hoax. There were no actors. No hidden wires. No rational explanations. Something had happened that shouldn't have been *able* to happen.

He now believed.

Rushing out of The Crooked Star, he had to get to his car.

The noises in the town had stopped, not that he was in any frame of mind to notice.

Rounding a corner at full speed, only a dozen feet from where his car had been parked, Trent slammed face-first into a wall.

No, not a wall, despite it feeling like it was. It was Styles.

Her fist connected with his face with such immense strength that he collapsed backward without her even moving an inch.

His world spun sideways, as the sidewalk grazed across his palms, and blood filled his mouth.

Above him, she loomed, laughing.

And behind her came the others.

Townspeople. Children. Dogs.

Each of them were the ones who had been

screaming in their houses moments before. They emerged from all corners of the shadowy streets, shifting toward him in the same sick, stuttering way. Their bodies contorted. Bones stuck out, too large for the skin that covered them. Mouths hung open wider than any jaw should. Large, serrated teeth smiling at Trent with a hungry glee. One child walked sideways on all fours, her head twisted around and facing forward, with all the bones in her neck snapped and reformed.

They had changed.

They had become.

They were now something ancient. Twisted and broken.

Their eyes faintly glowed in the dark, and their bodies twitched as they got closer.

Trent forced himself to his feet.

Styles giggled again. Holding her hand over her mouth, as if this were the funniest thing she had witnessed.

He didn't hesitate.

He hit her back.

Harder.

As hard as he possibly could.

His punch landed on the monstrous side of her face, and her body went instantly limp. No sound. No scream. She just fell to the ground like the power had been shut off.

In The Mouth of Madness

Without meeting the stares of the approaching townsfolk, he reached down and grabbed her body, lifting her under the arms. He dragged her across the pavement toward the car. Her arms were limp and swung with each step, as her shoes scraped along the concrete. The mutated townsfolk didn't move to stop him. They just moved in closer, staggering, watching in what seemed like an amused silence.

Trent got to the car, flung the door open with one hand, and shoved Styles inside. She collapsed into the passenger seat. Rushing around, he raced into the driver's seat, slamming the door behind him, trying to not look at the horrific things outside that stared in.

His hands fumbled at the ignition.

No keys.

They weren't in the dash. Not in his pocket. Not anywhere.

Panic twisted like a coiling spring.

"Come on, come on—" he muttered as he shut his eyes, thinking. "One and one is two... two and two is four... three and three is six... four and four is eight..."

The math calmed him. Barely. Enabled him to think somewhat clearer. He opened his eyes. Where did he leave the keys? In the hotel? Did he drop them in the bar?

Beside him, a giggle.

He turned.

Styles sat slumped in the seat, awake, grinning.

Her eyes were wet and misaligned, gazing nowhere and everywhere at once, as if seeing through him and around him. Her hand raised slowly, and there between her fingers were the keys. Jingling softly.

She opened her mouth, not just wide, but gaping, impossible, stretching down toward her chest. Without breaking eye contact, if it could still be called that, she dropped the keyring into her immense throat.

Trent jerked forward with a gasp, instinct overriding his disgust and horror. His hand dove into her mouth, disappearing past the sharp teeth dripping with drool. Her throat convulsed around his wrist as he reached deeper. Then, *crack*, her jaws snapped shut on his wrist like a bear trap.

Agony. He could feel the teeth break the skin, feel them scraping his bone. Still, he shoved deeper, fingers groping through pulsing flesh and slippery warmth.

"Give them to me!" he snarled in a panic.

Styles writhed beneath him, gurgling a sound that was part scream, part retching laughter.

The mutated mob pressed in closer. Surrounding the car, their fingers smeared over the glass, as they pushed their faces against the windows, watching Trent with cruel smiles on their contorted faces.

Trent screamed as he slammed Styles' face down onto the dashboard. Using his hand in her mouth to smash her into the plastic, over and over, until eventually, she lost consciousness. Her mouth loosened, letting him pull his arm out. Covered in bile and spit, yet now holding the keys.

Through the driver's side, a child stood staring in, face squashed against the window, eyes glowing, teeth sharp in display as her tongue slid across the glass, licking. More creature than human. More it than she. And it didn't blink.

Trent had to force his gaze away, as he shoved the key into the ignition.

The engine coughed once.

Then again.

And then, mercifully, it caught.

The moment the car sped forward, the things on the outside peeled away, their limbs flailing uselessly as they parted, allowing the vehicle to surge toward the covered bridge out of town.

As the car hit the road on the other side of the bridge, and as the town of Hobb's End disappeared in his rearview, Trent breathed easier.

Despite the monster that was Styles now knocked out in the passenger seat, he felt his panic subside the further away the town became.

It was still night. Still pitch black, and the only light was from the headlamps guiding the way.

Trent did not, *could not*, begin to think about what it all meant. He witnessed it. But what was it? Why was it?

. . .

Don't force this away, John Trent. Just accept.

No, *no,* he thought as his hands gripped the steering wheel.

He muttered, quietly at first. "Never leave the city. Never... why the hell don't I ever learn... Nothing out here but inbreeding. Never again... *never* again."

Styles stirred in the seat beside him. Her voice was slurred and sore. "Are we leaving?" she asked.

Turning to her with a sudden terrified expression, he quickly saw that the monster half of her body was gone. With a gash on her forehead from the collision with the dashboard, she looked like Styles again.

"We're going home," he said. More to comfort himself than her. Wary about her, but presuming whatever influence the town had on her, had now gone.

"Please, don't leave me," she whispered.

Time passed. How much, Trent didn't know. A mist had surrounded the road and grew thicker on the windscreen the further he drove.

Leaning forward, he wiped the condensation from the windshield with his hand.

"Where's the fucking highway?" he whispered, gripping the wheel tighter.

In The Mouth of Madness

There were no signs. No road markers. Nothing. This narrow road had gone on too long.

But up ahead, through the mist, Trent could see something.

The car slowed.

There, barely visible, was a phone booth.

There were no poles nearby. No wires. No connection to anything. But it glowed softly from within its glass shell. The phone box stood in the middle of nowhere like it had grown from the ground. But Trent saw none of the warning signs. He just saw the possible link to freedom.

He opened the door and rushed out, Styles just sat and watched, half in and out of sleep.

He looked around. There was nothing but the night and fog. Really nothing. No birds, no insects, no sounds in the distance. Just a void of noise. A suppressing silence.

"Call triple-A," he said to himself. "Call the cops. Call Mom. Call the Goddamn Ghostbusters..."

He laughed to himself in a sad, bittersweet way.

Checking his pockets for change, he brought out a few quarters in his palm.

But then, from behind on the narrow road, came a noise. A soft squeaking.

The kind of sound only a bicycle could make.

The change fell from his fingers, as he turned. Knowing exactly what, or more precisely who, he would see.

And there they were... Out of the fog came the boy. White-haired. Pedaling fast. He didn't look at Trent as he passed, he just kept on going. Just like before.

Then he was gone.

And the phone in the booth began to ring.

Trent backed away from it, slowly.

"Please, no."

Styles' voice came from behind, no longer slurring, as distorted as it was in the hotel room.

"He's got a job for you," she said with a perverse menace.

Trent turned to her.

He was not prepared to see. But he had no choice.

She was no longer standing.

She crawled toward him, spider-like, elbows twisted behind her, knees bent the wrong way. Her body scuttered forward, limbs splayed out, fingers digging into the dirt like claws. Her eyes rolled back, glowing a bright blue. Her mouth hung as wide as ever. Exposing her deep gullet.

Trent screamed and stepped on her, literally *stepped* on her, just to get past back to the car. His boots crunched the bones on her hand as he moved.

She hissed in anger, not pain.

The engine hadn't stopped running, and he was not stopping for her anymore.

He slammed his foot on the accelerator.

. . .

Trent drove in silence. Eyes forward. Face stoney.

Needing some distraction, he clicked on the radio and turned the dial slowly to find a station. But all there was, was white noise.

The same white noise from the phone.

The misty road ahead was flat. Straight. Endless.

In fact... He could only see the mist, because the road... The road wasn't there anymore.

Not the same road he was on.

It had now changed, as the mist drifted away.

The gravel shoulders were now sidewalks. The ground was not clear but littered with debris.

He slammed the brake, and the car screamed to a halt.

He stared ahead in disbelief.

Hobb's End.

He was back in Hobb's End.

Facing him, the large crowd of mutated townsfolk laughed manically at his arrival.

The wheels screamed as the car was forced violently in reverse, turning back the way he had come. With the same frantic desperation as a cornered animal, Trent sped away again, over the covered bridge and away from the town limits of Hobb's End.

He dared not even look back. He just drove as fast as he could. He could feel the stares behind him... the whole town. Watching him. Laughing at him.

"A few bad calls... a few wrong turns..." Trent

mumbled, trying to justify what had happened. "Road curled around, simple. Must have missed the turn-off."

He tried to laugh but found no humor in his words or the situation. He only found a dry, rising panic. He pushed the gas pedal down harder, like it could tear him free from whatever was behind him.

The narrow, rural road lay unnaturally straight before him, as the mist began to swirl around yet again.

Without warning, he saw the boy again.

The same boy.

Still pedaling the same bicycle in the same direction.

Only this time, he was even older. Much, much older.

He had looked like he had an old man's head on a young man's body, but now, the body was gnarled, the face even more ancient. His long white hair was more threadbare and exposed his liver-spotted head.

Overtaking the boy, Trent squinted, not wanting to see any more.

But it wasn't the old boy that made him scream, it was the burst of manic laughter that shattered the silence *inside* the vehicle. A laugh from his backseat.

Trent spun, instinctual and horrified.

Styles was sat there. Not herself. No longer human. What sat there was wearing her face like a costume, twisted into a smile that split her cheeks wide. Her laughter echoed like a chorus of many voices crammed into one mouth. Her eyes were wide and

In The Mouth of Madness

wild, glowing blue, filled with joy far too sick to be sane.

The car swerved, as the tires fought to hold onto the road. Styles clapped her twisted hands like a child on a carnival ride, delighted by his fear and panic.

The laughter then vanished as quickly as it had begun.

Silence.

Trent turned again. The backseat was empty.

Moisture had gathered on the windshield again.

He leaned forward, eyes straining, will ebbing.

And the veil lifted.

The mist thinned.

And there it was.

Hobb's End.

Again.

No way he could be back here. The road had been straight. But the town had returned to him. Waiting still. Laughing still.

But no one could be seen.

As the car came to a halt, Trent could hear the townsfolk, but no one was there. Not until, in the distance, movement stirred and began running toward the car.

Dogs.

Dozens of them. Rabid. Furious. Sprinting toward Trent in a mad, snarling pack. Their eyes glowed like Styles'.

Trent's foot hit the gas once, and the car flew into

another U-turn. The vehicle bucked, jolted, and sped away, leaving the dogs and the town behind him again.

Or so he prayed.

But this road was not about to offer an iota of mercy.

It was only a matter of minutes before the boy, in his even more decrepit, ancient state came into view. Pedaling in the same direction, though more frantically than before.

Only now, Styles was behind him, scurrying at impossible speed after him. A look of murderous rage plastered on her gaping face.

Trent didn't slow.

He couldn't question it.

He overtook them at full speed, and for the sake of his sanity, ignored that they were even there.

Maybe they weren't there, John Trent? Or maybe everything was.

The car raced forward, as the engine cried a constant, revving howl.

Inside, Trent's expression sagged. His terror had thinned out into total exhaustion. Apathy. Mentally, physically, he felt like a broken man.

That is why he didn't even flinch when Hobb's End came into view once more.

In The Mouth of Madness

He pulled in slowly this time, headlights shining over the townsfolk who were stood there again. The dogs too. There, motionless, glaring at him as he arrived. No more laughter. Just horribly grinning faces that were now lit in the glare of the car's headlamps. They did not move. They did not speak. They just watched him, looking like statues.

Trent tightened his hold on the steering wheel. A grim smile broke over his face.

If they wanted a war, he'd give them one.

"Not today," he said as he floored the pedal.

Then, without warning, *she* appeared.

Styles.

Right in front of him.

Alive.

Whole.

Not monstrous.

Right at the front of the crowd, in the path of the car, smiling happily.

Trent didn't have time to think, only to react, out of reflex more than thought.

He yanked the wheel to the right.

The tires cried out in protest as they lost grip.

Steel met steel with a deafening smash as the car slammed into another parked vehicle. The impact threw Trent forward. His head hit the steering wheel with a terrible force...

...Then there was darkness.

And silence.

No Styles.
No mob.
No laughter.
Just Trent's unconscious body slumped in the seat, bleeding from his broken nose.

Chapter Eight

The black church stood almost invisible against the dark featureless expanse of the night sky. There was no light here, the moon had gone, the stars had stopped shining. Outside on the front steps, the children from the town, along with the dogs, sat and stared ahead. In their hideously transformed bodies, they now waited. On guard.

In the town the other monsters roamed the streets. Aimless. Waiting.

Inside the church, John Trent was sat in one of the confessional booths. Terrified, shaking, as the lightbulb above him flickered like it could give out at any moment. Grabbing one of the last cigarettes from the pack in his jacket, he tried his best to light it, but there was no lighter in his pocket. He had dropped it in the bar.

Only a few moments ago, he had come to in the booth, his nose throbbing in pain, with an almost blinding headache.

Of course, he had tried the door, to get out and run, but it was immovable. Not locked. The door was just shut and did not open. He was trapped. And all he wanted right now was a smoke.

From the partition wall to Trent's side, a voice came through. Calm, low and matter of fact. At total odds with everything that had happened here.

It was Sutter Cane.

"Do you want to know the problem with places like this?" the voice asked. "With religion in general? Not any religion. All religion."

Trent's lip curled in annoyance. "I'm guessing you're going to tell me," he said flippantly. Sure, he was scared. Sure, he wanted out. But the last thing he wanted was to engage in small talk with the ringmaster of this whole thing.

"These religions never know how to convey the true anatomy of horror," Cane said. His tone held no malice, just a certainty as if reciting a lecture. "Religions that humanity created seek discipline through fear, yet none of them understand the very nature of the creation that spawned them. You see, no one's ever believed it enough to make it all real. Not really... The same cannot be said of my work."

Trent balled up the unlit cigarette in his fist and threw it to his feet. "So, you're saying you're a better god than God, huh?"

"Not at all," Cane replied, sounding quite delighted at Trent's words. "I'm saying I'm the only one who ever bothered to show up."

"Your work isn't real," Trent said, pointedly. "None of this is real. This is something else."

"What is it then?" Cane asked.

"You're just a fiction writer who bought into his own bullshit along with some psycho fans. This is mass hysteria. This is a big cult. It can't be real... *It can't be.*"

"You know you don't think that, it is just easier to say it isn't real than admit out loud what you cannot comprehend," Cane said softly.

"I don't *want* to believe what I saw," Trent said, not sounding that sure in his words. Trying his best to remain calm. "I *don't want* to. But I saw a guy turn into a fucking octopus and blow his own face off. What does that mean? I saw your agent gunned down. I saw Mrs. Pickman... It *can't* be real..." His words fell away.

Cane leaned in closer to the lattice partition. "I came out here and found something that had only ever existed in my imagination. Until they found *me*. I had to accept them too, after much denial. But in the end. I saw them. I saw them as they were. You see, you need my book to see it, and once you see it, you *become* it. All those years thinking it was just my dreams, not realizing *they* were telling me what to write. I was not the writer. I was their herald. So, don't feel bad that you witness yet cannot see."

"They wrote your books? If you don't mind me saying, *they* did a shitty job."

Cane chuckled. "You sound calm for a man who's seen what you have seen tonight. Most minds would come undone at a fraction of the sights. I suppose I should credit myself for that. And you saw a lot tonight, didn't you?"

"*It can't be fucking real!*" Trent's voice reverberated inside the booth. "Your book are not real."

He closed his eyes and forced himself to steady his breathing and try to block out the memories of the night.

Cane laughed. "Well, if you didn't like them, you really must try my new one," he said. "It will drive you absolutely mad."

"Fuck you," Trent replied weakly. Taking a deep breath.

"John, you must understand why this is happening. The books... They prepare you. Just like it has here. It makes you ready. Prepares your mind for them to walk in. You could say that with the people here, that we have had a very successful test market... And now... Now it's ready for the world... It will become the last bestseller of humanity, and you... You are the main character."

Trent didn't reply. Not even trying to argue

anymore. He just sat quietly, resigned as he listened to Cane's diatribe.

"It's not modesty when I say that I am very, very popular. After only six books, my sales eclipse the holy writings of every single religion together." Then, with a whisper of glee, "I guess you could say that I am the new religion... But do not get me wrong. I am not the god. I am merely the conduit... Now, let me show you something.

Without warning, two arms burst through the partition and grabbed Trent by the throat, lifted him with immense ease, and *slammed* his face into the wooden door in front of him.

* * *

Trent woke with a gasp, slumped in a chair in the impossibly expansive attic of the church.

A cloth was being pressed gently against his forehead.

He flinched as he heard a voice.

Styles.

"You promised not to leave me," she said.

"Linda?" he whispered, looking up at her human face. No trace of anything, not even the gash on her forehead remained.

"You broke your word," she said. "And let him hurt me..."

Trent's mind pushed the image of her spider-like

form down, deep down, locking it in the mental box with all the other things he refused to accept.

"Where is he?" he asked, his voice a whisper.

She smiled as she stepped aside. "He's finishing."

There, Cane was at his table. He too was also in total human form. No monstrous side revealed.

Behind his desk, at the far back where the wall should be, there was a long wide mark hanging in the air. A tear. A rip in the darkness around it. Torn like paper across the shadows, peeling open. Through this gaping wound, from inside, came a blackness too dark to fathom.

Cane continued to type, his fingers dancing across the keys. And every stroke, every stamp of a letter on the paper, the floating breach behind him, seemed to widen more and more.

"He's letting them back in," Styles said, reverently, staring at Cane with a smile of joy.

Trent painfully got out of the chair, but as he did, a strong wind billowed toward him from inside of the rip and pushed at him, as if trying to keep him away. It carried no noise. No howls. It was silent, aside from the clacking of the typewriter.

He turned to Styles, but she had gone. Vanished as soon as the wind arrived.

With a flurry of final words, Cane's smile grew and grew, as the speed of his words increased. He appeared more gleeful by the moment, until eventually he pulled

In The Mouth of Madness

the page from the typewriter, and held it up with almost paternal pride.

"And it is *finally* done," he exclaimed, laying the single sheet on top of the stack of papers next to him. The gusting wind somehow did not affect him, nor did it even move a single hair on his head. It only hit Trent. Pushing at him. Keeping him at bay.

"*In The Mouth of Madness,*" Cane said with a toothy smile, "And it is yours to deliver, John Trent."

Trent wanted to shout *What the fuck are you talking about?* But he was struggling against the wind. Trying to get closer. *Needing* to get closer. All he wanted to do was grab Cane by the collar and demand to know the truth. None of this was real. It couldn't be... It couldn't be... *It couldn't be...*

"Where is Styles," he demanded loudly.

Shhh, John Trent. Just listen.

Cane stood from the desk. "She is not here now. She has no place." He looked down at the manuscript thoughtfully. "Can you fathom the pressure of having to write the last book?"

Now nearer, having fought against the silent wind, Trent managed to grab onto the desk. He looked at Cane aghast. "You're going to make everyone read this and it will kill them? Do you know how fucking insane that sounds?"

"Kill? No John Trent. Death is subjective. Yes, many will cease in their form, but the rest will change. Evolve. The chosen shall embrace the madness like a warm blanket."

Trent stared at him, then behind, at the rip that hung in the air.

"You want to know about what is in there?" Cane asked, gesturing toward the impossible space. "Well, I'll be joining my new publishers in there... but you... you'll take this book. You'll deliver it. For you are my prophet... and it is what you do... What your purpose is."

"What *I* do?"

"You still don't realize, *do you*? My book does not replace your world, it *becomes* your world. And you... You work in it."

"*No*," Trent grimaced, gradually losing his grip on the table as the silent wind blew harder against him. "I know *what* I am. I know what's *real*!"

Cane laughed loudly, as his eyes shimmered in a blue glow. "You are what I write and nothing more... Do you think my agent chose you by accident?"

"They chose the *company*."

Cane's laughter continued. "No, I just wrote it that way. I wrote that Arcane was a long-standing client of your insurance company... which did not even exist

In The Mouth of Madness

before I tapped the keys to form the words... So... it became... Now you will hand my new reality unto that world."

Trent's mind reeled. He tried to remember. Robinson. The company. But before...

"Tell me this... What is your mother's name?" Cane asked.

Trent had nothing.

"Or your father's?"

Nothing.

"Where were you born?"

Trent gasped. He remembered none of it.

Cane spoke slowly. "Arthur and Lois Cane. Their baby boy Jonathan was born in the back of a station wagon on the side of the Brooklyn-Queens Expressway."

Suddenly Trent remembered all of that. As if he had always known it.

"I wrote you. You're mine... But if I had to do it again, I'd make you smoke less. It's a writer's crutch I just can't shake. The descriptors run dry... there's only so many times I can say you gasped, froze, mumbled, stared. I always fall back on the cigarette. It's funny, really. The man who wrote the final book... still hasn't mastered it. Quite an irony."

"I'm *not* a piece of fiction," Trent screamed. The wind continuing to beat at him.

Leering, Cane pointed to his own head. "I think,"

he said. "Therefore, *you are.*" He reached down and held up the manuscript. "You are in here John. All that you are and all that you know. If you do not believe me, read it."

Behind him, the rip was growing wider.

Trent's mind was fracturing. All he could say, all he could ask was.... "*Why?*"

"Only something not from reality can deliver the gospel unto the world."

At that moment, a chorus of large terrifying roars and growls seeped out from the expanding rip. Noises from beings so monstrous that they defied the instincts of even the oldest parts of the human brain. These were not sounds meant for ears. They were the vocalizations of concepts, of hunger that never knew satisfaction, of pain that had outlived its purpose, of languages dead before the Earth had cooled. There was no rhythm to their calls, only a vast chaos. And in that void beyond the breach, they were getting closer. Colossal, abstract, and impossible. Shapes that squirmed and writhed, crawled and clambered, with forms that resembled fang, death and thought, all at once. Their skin, their tentacles, and their claws, all shimmered with colors that hadn't been seen for an eternity. Their eyes, where each had some, none or a litany, stared out with emotion, but with intent. They were not just monsters. They were the beasts that created the very existence that banished them.

They were getting closer and closer.

And in an instant, Cane was stood in front of Trent, appearing closer to him in a heartbeat. With the wind still not affecting him, he grabbed Trent by the collar and lifted him up high.

"Spread the word," Cane grinned, then threw Trent across the room, as though he did not weigh a thing.

Trent came smashing out of the steeple window. He crashed onto the sloped roof of the church, bounced once, hard, and tumbled down onto the grass below. Landing with an almighty thud.

It should have killed him on impact.

The fall was over a hundred foot of a sheer drop onto a solid ground.

Yet he lay there on the grass. His body screamed in protest, ribs tight, lungs burning... But he was alive and able to get to his feet. Nothing was broken at all. Even his nose, which smashed in the crash, was fine now. No wounds. Just an all-over aching.

He turned, staggering backward, as his eyes locked on the steeple above, just as the top of it burst wide open. Not with fire or light, but with the impossible darkness, deeper than shadows, spilling from within. Against the night, what came out was so much darker. Spilling like oil across the sky, swallowing everything it touched.

Still sitting on the steps, the children and dogs just

stared at the sky, ignoring Trent completely, as the whole church started to groan.

The steeple started to sag inwards as the darkness started to widen from inside, breaking the whole building apart. The glass shattered, as the stone and wood of its structure cracked and crumbled.

Then, from each of their mouths and eyes, the darkness shot out of the children and the dogs. Screaming up to the sky to assist in blotting it out.

Trent ran... But he could not escape it. The same sounds soon erupted from all of the buildings as he passed them, and they too cracked open, letting loose a torrent of the void upward.

The people too. Each twisted and malformed thing was now stood still, as the darkness shot out from inside, escaping through their eyes and mouths, shooting upwards.

Trent kept running, as everything around him was breaking apart.

As the buildings cracked open, they also began to lose their color and turn brittle, collapsing to dust beneath the weight of the darkness escaping from them. It happened to the people too, as their bodies dissolved and soon became nothing.

Even the ground beneath his feet began to grow grayer and start to crack.

He ran harder, lungs scraping against his chest. He could hear his heartbeat, loud and erratic.

In The Mouth of Madness

His car came into view... dented but still in one piece.

He got in and yanked the door shut and started the engine with shaking hands. The key turned. The motor roared.

Looking out of the windscreen, he could see the sky above had now twisted in on itself, the clouds warped and curled like they were being pulled down a drain.

The void wasn't moving fast, it didn't need to. It simply advanced, inevitably touching everything in its path, like a crawling slick.

The church was gone, and Hobb's End was collapsing.

He slammed the car into gear and left nothing but burned rubber.

As he sped away, the darkness followed him.

He should have known better. He could not escape before, what made him think it would be any different now?

Like a slow wave, it stretched across the hills and into the trees, destroying everything it touched. And from within the darkness all around, even from this distance, Trent could hear the roars and growls. The same ones from the steeple. But now they were larger. Much, much larger.

Trying to quell his fears, Trent saw something out of the corner of his eye.

Sutter Cane

There on the passenger seat, lying innocuously was a grey box, with the words *In The Mouth of Madness* written in marker on the top.

Before he could think of how it got there, as the car listed to one side, hitting the gravel on the roadside, he peered up—

"Shit," was all he could mutter as the car slammed headfirst into a tree.

The impact was immense.

Loud.

Devastating.

The car crumpled against the old trunk and was stopped dead. Trent's body was hurled forward, as he smashed into the wheel.

John, I'm sorry... I could not resist.

A warming sunlight pushed through the darkness of the departing storm clouds, as it caught the broken glass of the windshield, casting its light across the interior of the wreck. The car was totaled. Crumpled. Wrapped around the thick base of the tree that had ended Trent's escape. But now, the events of the previous night were gone. The encroaching void nowhere to be seen. The devastation it wrought was nothing but a memory. The surrounding plant life was

In The Mouth of Madness

still alive, not consumed and drained as it was in Hobb's End.

Trent stirred in the driver's seat, groaning. But like before, somehow, he was alive and in one piece. No broken bones. No blood. Just the ache.

His eyes were bleary, and he took a long breath. He had to squint as his eyes adjusted to the glare of the sun high above.

Pushing the driver's side door open, he climbed out slowly. His legs were stiff and his back was sore, but he was in one piece. From looking at the damage to the car, there was no way he should be able to stand, let alone breathe.

The front end had folded around the trunk like the very metal had tried to embrace it. And right as he was looking at it, the tree creaked ominously. Its very core was fractured from the impact.

There was nothing much Trent could do. He could not fix the car. Not like AAA could come and patch it up... Not only that but he had no clue where he was and could not see anywhere a phone may be. So, he turned away, his face blank, and started walking down the road, in the direction that he thought he was driving in.

As he paced down the side of the road, with comedic timing, the tree behind him let out a long groan, and cracked in half. The thick trunk split as the top half collapsed forward toppling down onto the remnants of the car, crushing all that remained beneath it.

Trent didn't flinch, he just let out a small laugh, turned and continued his journey on foot.

He could not work out much about what happened to him. Every time he tried, he got too confused. He was in no state to try and make sense of something that made no sense. So, he just walked.

He wanted a cigarette but kept thinking about what Cane had said. That he *wrote* that in.

As an act of defiance, Trent did not walk back to the car to check the car lighter, to see if it would work. He just carried on. Not smoking...

"Fuck you Cane," he muttered.

The road stretched on, gray and cracked, bordered by silence and desolation.

Then came that sound.

High-pitched. Repetitive.

A soft rhythm growing louder behind him. A bicycle.

His stomach fell. "Please, God, no," he said under his breath, but as he turned, he felt relieved. It was still a teenage boy on a pedal bike, but not the one from Hobb's End. This one wore a backpack bulging with rolled newspapers. The tires of his bike squeaked with each rotation.

"Hey, kid," Trent called out.

In The Mouth of Madness

The boy slowed his bike to a stop.

"You want a paper, mister?" he asked.

Trent stared for a moment. No reply.

"Mister, are you okay?" the boy asked, looking warily.

Trent had no idea what he could say. What he *should* say. And all that came out was something he had no control over.

"I'm... a book, apparently," he said softly. "I thought I was from Brooklyn, but I'm... actually... a book. A horror book."

"Huh?" the boy said.

Trent laughed without finding any of it funny. "Yeah, I'm a book that drives people insane... and turns them into big ol' monsters."

The boy blinked.

"You been in an accident or something?" he asked. "Bump your head?"

Trent nodded slowly as tears started to fall. "Yeah, I have."

"You want me to get somebody? Call a doc?"

Trent tried to contain his emotion, but it was now coming out in force.

"Can you just tell me where the highway is?" he blubbed.

The boy pointed ahead.

"Straight up about ten miles. You're going the right way... Are you *sure* you're okay?"

Trent nodded, though still cried.

Looking a bit perturbed, the boy started to pedal away.

"Hey," Trent called out after him.

The boy glanced back, still pedaling.

"You ever hear of a place called Hobb's End?"

The boy shook his head and continued on his way, tires squeaking as he carried on down the road.

An hour passed and Trent was still walking. The tears though had stopped. Now he just felt empty.

Sweat gathered beneath his shirt as the sun beat down hot. His mouth was dry, and a cigarette hung from his lips, unlit. He couldn't be bothered to fight it, even if he had no light on him. So it just was in his mouth as the next best thing.

The highway came into view sometime later, a long gray artery stretching across the heat-blurred landscape. The further he walked, the more greenery had spread either side of him. And then he saw something that made him almost start jumping for joy. Traffic. Other people. Driving on their journeys. Welcoming the normality, he smiled.

Stepping up onto the shoulder, he raised his thumb as the cars shot by.

It was about another ten minutes of people ignoring his plea until a truck pulled over, willing to take on a hitchhiker.

Trent, smiling, climbed in. Happy to get off his aching feet.

The driver was massive. A broad slab of a meaty man, belly spilling over his belt, arms thick as thighs. His fingers wrapped around the wheel like oversized sausages.

"Where ya headed, hoss?" the man drawled in a Southern accent.

"New York?"

The driver smiled. "You're quite far out, but lucky for you, I'm headin' to Jersey, so'll pass right by. I could do with the company too."

Trent nodded with an appreciative smile.

The driver continued. "Whattaya do in the big apple?"

Trent glanced out to the road ahead of them. He thought for a second, and before he could say that he was an insurance claims investigator, he instead blurted. "I've been told that I'm a book. You're in it too, I guess..." He had no idea why he said that again. He did not mean to.

"Uhhh, what?"

Trent was back on the shoulder of the highway within seconds. He did not protest or ask any questions. He just stepped down from the truck and shut the door behind him. He wished he had asked the driver for a light...

The truck soon disappeared into the distance without another word.

"What the fuck?" he muttered, unsure of himself.

* * *

Just as the sun began to set, and after another three hours of walking, with no more people willing to give him a ride, Trent felt an immense wave of happiness as the roadside motel came into view.

It was the kind of place built for guests who wanted to remain anonymous. Low, rectangular, with a flickering sign that had long since stopped spelling its full name. What had once been *The Gillman House Motel*, was now *Te Gim Hose Motl*. It bled a soft pink neon light onto the darkening parking lot and hummed like it was slowly dying.

All he could think of was, finally, he would be able to have a cigarette.

The room was sparse and smelled of bad decisions. He did not care though.

He lay across the bed fully dressed, one arm draped across his stomach, the other holding the room's telephone. A lit cigarette finally between his teeth, and the warming smoke filled his lungs and settled the last of his nerves.

"Fuck you, Cane,' he muttered again.

In The Mouth of Madness

In front of him, the television shone out grainy infomercial after infomercial, and above him, a ceiling fan spun in tired, uneven circles.

He picked up the receiver and dialed.

It rang, but there was no answer.

In Jackson Harglow's office at Arcane Publishing, the lights were off, and the room was empty. Of course it was. The wall clock ticked over to 10 p.m. and just as it should be, everything was quiet.

Trent hung up. He let the phone rest back into its cradle.

Taking another long drag, he pushed himself up and off the bed.

The shower was on, the water was hot. Steam collected along the edges of the mirror, beginning to take it over, as Trent stood naked and wet, staring at his reflection. The light over the mirror was bright enough to reveal the fatigue that was set deep into his face. He looked older. Not wiser. Not graceful. Just different. Worn. Beaten.

. . .

Sutter Cane

That night, Trent slept, though not well. He was fully dressed again in his dirty clothes, with his boots laced, on top of the covers. The lights in the motel room remained switched on. The television too, with its volume turned low.

He dreamed about his parents, Arthur and Lois.

And even in those dreams, he did not trust who they were. *What* they were. Especially when Sutter Cane showed up to lecture him again.

The next morning, walking into the reception to check out, Trent was immediately hit with the welcoming smell of freshly brewed coffee and artificial pine.

Walking straight over to the cigarette machine, he pulled out a handful of coins from his pocket and got himself a fresh pack.

He may have lost his bag, his change of clothes, but at least he had his wallet and some cash.

A young clerk in a red motel polo walked in from a back office to behind the reception desk. She perked up at the sight of him.

"Mr. Trent?" she asked.

He grabbed his cigarette pack from the slot, and turned to her.

"There's a package for you, sir," she said with a smile.

The parcel she slid across the desk was unmarked,

thick, stamped only with Trent's name. No return address. Trent didn't move.

"No one knows I'm here."

She shrugged. "Well, someone sure does."

In his room, a game show was playing on the television, as he lit up another cigarette.

"Fuck you, Cane," he said again before taking the first drag. His new mantra.

He was sat at the table in front of the package.

He knew what was in there but had to see for sure.

His gaze stayed fixed on it, as he smoked at least half of the cigarette before mustering the nerve to look inside.

A sudden rap at the door made him flinch.

"Housekeeping," came the muffled, heavily Latino-accent.

"Not now," Trent shouted back.

He heard the footsteps move to the next room, pushing the trolly with them.

Picking up the parcel he began to tear open the packaging. His nervous fingers making it a much slower process.

And there it was... clean, clipped and neatly stacked.

The manuscript. *In the Mouth of Madness.*

He stared at it for a long time. And the longer he stared, the angrier he became.

. . .

Back in the lobby, the clerk barely had time to register his presence before Trent was there, one hand gripping the front of her shirt, wrenching her half over the countertop.

"*Who delivered this?*" Trent hissed, holding the manuscript up between them.

The clerk squirmed, wide-eyed. "I... I don't know—"

"*Who?!*"

"I wasn't even here last night!"

"Then who was?"

A voice boomed from the office behind the desk, deep and heavy.

"I was."

A large woman stepped forward. Broad and stern. "And I didn't see shit. So let the girl go."

Trent quickly released his grip, realizing his misplaced frustration. The clerk slumped back.

"Leave now, before I call the cops," the woman ordered. "You understand?"

He did.

Before he left the lobby, he threw the manuscript into the trash can by the door.

After a short walk into the nearby town, Trent had waited another six cigarettes for the bus. This was his

In The Mouth of Madness

only option. There were no airports, no taxis, no car hire firms. So, he stood for hours, smoking away the boredom.

By the time the afternoon came, the bus was headed for New York City, roaring down the highway.

Trent was sat by the window. Beside him the seat was occupied by an octogenarian woman who looked as if she were made purely out of bone and leathery skin. An obvious wig of bright orange hair sat on her head, styled more akin to a clown than to any known fashion. She was in the middle of a monologue that had no real beginning, and had already been talking *at* Trent for nearly twenty minutes. He tried his best to not engage. He didn't look in her direction, nor reply to her, but nothing he did had dissuaded the non-sequitur laced story from falling out of her mouth.

"I remember New York during the depression, you know," she said, in a voice that was high-pitched and cracked. "People think they have it bad now, you should've seen the Bowery back then. Bodies piled two, three feet high off the gutter, and not all of 'em were dead yet either." She paused, her cloudy eyes looking around as if recalling her story. "Cold," she whispered. "That's what did most of 'em in. Cold, and no one to care for 'em."

Trent wanted to sleep. Would she even notice, or care if he did?

"They used to call me Little Mags back then," she said suddenly, her eyes sharper, a flicker of mischief rushing behind them. "Ran messages for the dockworkers. Ran numbers, too, when things got lean. You had to be quick, and quiet. And I was both." She laughed at what she said, despite none of it being humorous.

Trent took a deep breath in and just closed his eyes. He would drift away from this banality. He did not want to hear any more of it.

But she continued, nevertheless. "One night, winter of 33 I think, I saw a man steal another man's coat right off his back. Shot him in the knee first mind you. Didn't even bother to run. Just walked away happy that he had another layer to keep him warm. Of course, the cops didn't care. They never did down there. *That* was the Bowery. City let it rot."

Her voice slowly faded away.

Trent thought he was finally falling asleep.

But the voice did not fade into silence exactly, but into absence. Opening his eyes again he turned at the old lady. Her mouth had kept moving, but the words were not reaching him.

He must be asleep. He *must* be.

By midnight, everything was dark. The lights along the aisles were all off and every passenger slept. Heads tilted, mouths open, bodies slack.

The driver sat alone in the front, headphones on, blocking out the sounds of snoring and wheezing.

In his seat, Trent stirred.

He could only have been out for a short time, but it had felt like a week. He was groggy, and for a moment had completely forgotten about Hobb's End. About the monsters. About Sutter *goddamn* Cane.

The further he got away from that town, the less any of it seemed real. He knew that he had witnessed some impossible things, where at the time he had no other recourse than to accept what was in front of him. But on this bus, he did not feel the same certainty. What about Styles?

His thoughts quickly began to change. Not what was being said, but how he heard them. Gone was the voice in his head, and instead it became something else. Something clear. It was not in his head. But next to him.

That voice.

"John Trent had started to doubt everything. Was Styles even real? Or just a character Cane created? He would investigate her when he got back to the city. He would investigate the whole of Arcane Publishing and get to the bottom of the Sutter Cane nonsense."

Cane was sat where the old lady had been.

He stared at Trent with a smile.

"Personally, John, I would not categorize any of this as nonsense," he said. "But I guess it's very *you* to think that."

Trent tried to speak, but could not. No word came out. He tried again. Nothing.

Cane continued. "I have written you some lines,

but they are not for now... In a moment." He turned and glanced around the bus. "It is amazing how ants seem so important up close isn't it? But when you know what they truly are, you see the sheer insignificance of their birth." He looked back to Trent, and as he spoke his voice started to fragment into different pitches layered on top of one another. Like a myriad of voices speaking at once.

"Wait until you get to the end, John," he said. "*That* is something else."

Trent held his breath as he clamped his eyes shut. Trying to wake himself up from this insanity.

When he opened them again, Cane was still there.

"I'm not going anywhere, John," he said. "I'm God now. Do you understand? I am everywhere at once."

Trent's reply came, low and bitter. "God's not supposed to be a hack horror writer."

Cane smiled. "I love that line, a bit of self-deprecation on my part." He took a long breath in before continuing. "You know you will never see the truth, unless you read the book. It's not all big monsters, you know? It's all a metaphor. The darkness too. A metaphor you will deliver."

He paused and motioned to Trent. "It's you're line now."

"You can't make me," Trent replied, finally able to talk.

"Oh, I can. I just don't want to spoil the ending... So instead... Maybe I can help you." He tilted his head to one side as he thought. "Look around when you wake up, really look... can you promise me that?"

Trent didn't answer.

"Did I ever tell you my favorite color was blue?"

Trent jolted awake, panicked and sweaty, having had the most vivid and terrible dream. He immediately looked around, wide-eyed, scanning the bus.

He could not believe what was there.

Everything was blue.

Everything.

The upholstery. The floor. The curtains. The outside vista. The other passengers. Blue hats. Blue coats. Blue shirts. Blue trees. Blue skin. Even the woman beside him, her previously orange hair now a brittle shade of blue. His own jacket, once grey, was blue too.

He gasped. Once, twice, and he fell back into his seat.

And then... then he screamed.

He screamed and it wouldn't stop.

The bus had to pull onto the hard shoulder so the driver could see what was going on. The old lady next to him stared worriedly at Trent, as she had one hand on his shoulder, trying to calm him down.

Trent had his fingers dug so far into his seat that his nails had torn the fabric. His eyes were terrified and he was dripping in sweat. Still screaming.

"Relax buddy," the driver said, stood in the aisle next to the seat. "You're awake now... Please calm down."

Trent looked at him as the screams started to die out, but in their place came tears. Floods of them like before.

"Oh, dearie," the old lady said. "It was just a bad dream. My momma used to tell me that bad dreams are just stories your mind tells when it's tired. Like little thunderstorms in your sleep. They pass. They always pass. Just hold on tight 'til morning, and they'll blow away like smoke."

Chapter Nine

The Department of Records and Information Services was buried deep in the belly of the old Providence Municipal Archives building. Its façade was more like a library than a governmental facility. Inside, the noise of the city gave way to a dry, reverential silence, broken only by the soft whir of scanners and the occasional metallic squeak of a rolling cart full of documents.

Trent, having left the bus, the old lady and all the blue coloring, had made it as far as Rhode Island. He decided that before he got on a bus again, he needed to look for some answers. And here he was, standing at the counter, facing a very old woman who looked like she'd been laminated decades ago and pulled back into circulation. Her hair was high, piled in the manner of a distant decade. Her sweater was tan, her lips a shade of coral not seen since Eisenhower, and her name tag,

MARJORIE, was pinned proudly like a medal. She was obviously not a woman who suffered fools gladly, or anyone else for that matter. She looked like joy was not a piece of her existence. All there was in her life was this job.

Behind her, rows of cabinets lined the walls, along with a large microfiche machine. Labeled box files lined the shelves that reached up higher than anyone could reach. The room was cold. Not unpleasantly so, just an unwelcoming temperature.

"I'm looking for a town," Trent said, holding out the paper with the name on it. "Hobb's End. It's somewhere in New England. North of Maine. I got the co-ordinates."

Marjorie didn't reach for the paper. She just glanced down at it, then up at Trent, then back down again. She looked unimpressed and frankly annoyed at being asked.

"Hobb's End?" she repeated, flatly. "I've never heard of it."

"I was just there," he explained, not raising his voice but accidentally letting an edge of annoyance creep into his words. "It's *real*. I walked the streets. There were loads of houses. A post office. A bar... It was called The Crooked Star. A church. People. Children. I stayed in the Pickman hotel." He tried to explain, to convince, but all he got back was a tight, polite smile. The kind city workers were trained to perfect.

In The Mouth of Madness

"One moment," she said, as she grabbed the piece of paper, and walked back over to a computer terminal behind her. "We've got land records going back to the Dutch. If it was ever there, we'd know about it."

The monitor flickered with a deep green prompt, the cursor blinking like a tiny heartbeat. Her fingers tapped on the keyboard, sounding as bored as she looked.

"H. O. B. B. S. or H. O. B. B. E. S.?"

"No E," he replied.

She entered the search term and hit the return button.

A few lines of data flashed up on the screen. Words he could not read from where he stood, but Marjorie could.

She picked up the slip of paper and typed in the coordinates. Hitting enter, the data found flashed up on the screen as before.

"As I thought. No municipal records in our archives," she said, walking back over to the reception desk. "No post office registration, no census tags, no zoning information. No plats, no permits. Not in Maine, not in Massachusetts, not in Vermont, not in New Hampshire."

She stared with a raised eyebrow. "Are you sure it wasn't called something else? People misremember things all the time. Bobs End? Jobs End? Hobbsville?"

"I remember the name fine," he said. "I didn't dream it. What about the co-ordinates?"

"Private farmland. No town."

"For fuck's sake." He was exasperated. Not at her, but at the situation, though she took his swearing personally.

She regarded him with a disapproving grimace. "Sir, we've had folks come in before chasing ghost towns," she said. "Old settlements, mining camps, places swallowed up by the woods. But there's always *something* to find. No matter how obscure. A record. A footprint. Hobb's End? It doesn't exist. Plain and simple. No ifs, ands or buts."

He didn't reply. Why was he not surprised? Why did he think it *would* be on a map. Of course, it wouldn't.

"Sometimes towns vanish," she said. "Get absorbed, renamed, wiped out by storms or floods or worse. But even then, there's residue. This one... there's nothing."

Marjorie then reached into a drawer and pulled out a small form, and slid it across the desk toward him.

"If you want to file a formal inquiry, you can," she said. "We'll search the hardcopy archives, but I'm telling you now, you won't find anything under that name or those coordinates."

Trent didn't pick up the paper.

Because he knew she was right.

And he knew, somewhere, Cane was laughing at him for even trying.

***

He felt lucky that the bus Providence to New York City was mostly empty, and he didn't have anyone reciting their life story to him. So, for the four-hour journey, Trent stared out of the window, watching the world pass him by. And as the wheels hit the New Jersey Turnpike, then entered the Lincoln Tunnel, he felt like the horror was over. He was almost home. He could not help but smile in relief and let out a chuckle.

A few minutes later, the bus hissed to a halt beneath the low ceiling of the Port Authority terminal. It had arrived on time at 7:49 p.m. and one by one, all the passengers filed out. No chatter. Just the noise of shuffling feet and the hydraulic hiss of the opening door.

Trent stepped off rumpled but composed. He took a deep breath in. The air was stale, humid, and stank of engine grease, damp clothing and human piss. Ah, New York City. *His* city.

He scanned the terminal before moving toward the main corridor. Normally familiar territory, but now something was amiss. The lighting was overly bright. The floor felt uneven beneath his feet. And the people, they were off too.

Slumped, lining both walls of the tunnel out was an abundance of derelicts and junkies. All huddled. Their clothing was torn and filthy and the further

Trent went, the worse they all seemed. And even worse, they all looked at him as he hurried by.

He tried not to look back at them, but that failed almost immediately.

One had the skin tone of curdled milk, pocked with red lesions that trailed up the side of their face and neck. Another's eyes bled as they smiled a mouthful of rotten teeth.

There was something off-kilter in their posture. Not random. Not drugged. Not despairing. These were not people who had given up.

One woman's head was mottled with scabs and pustules, as her hair fell away in uneven clumps. Her expression was fixed in glee as she noticed Trent pass.

He glanced back at her, at all of them, as he got to the end of the tunnel. Needing to get out, he turned, immediately colliding with a man in uniform. A transit cop.

The officer steadied Trent with his hand, the other gripping the leash of a large, stone-eyed German Shepherd. The dog was already sniffing at Trent's jacket.

"You alright, man?" the officer asked.

Trent didn't answer. He looked down at the dog, then to the cop's face.

But the cop's face was not normal.

It was Cane.

"Welcome home, John," he said with a smile.

Trent did not think. His emotions exploded as

violence. He struck the officer across the jaw with his fist, then snarled in anger as he threw another punch straight into his gut.

It was only a matter of moments before multiple hands grabbed Trent from every direction.

As the German Shepherd barked, Trent felt the nightstick smashing into his gut.

He was dragged down hard and pinned by three other officers, one shouting orders, another reaching for cuffs.

The officer he'd attacked clutched his face and cursed.

He was no longer Cane.

Within the hour, Trent was stood at the release desk while a bored police officer returned his personal effects without comment. A wallet. A pen. A lighter. Some loose change. Nothing else.

Behind the counter, two more officers sat at their desks. One flipped through a paperback with a cracked spine. The cover was familiar. The title clear. *The Hobb's End Horror*.

And the other officer was reading the same book.

Neither looked up at him.

Trent said nothing. He had been let off with a warning and a fine, and felt the need to keep his head down, get out and get home.

He slid his items into his coat, signed the form and left the police station without a sound.

The subway platform at DeKalb Avenue station was almost empty. A few commuters were here, keeping themselves to themselves.

Trent stood near the edge of the platform, not close, but enough to feel the wind come down the tunnels as the trains approached. He considered for a small moment about jumping. Hitting the live rail. Have the world solved in a second.

Look behind you.

Turning, Trent noticed the wall was lined with posters. Advertisements for brands that didn't matter. But some stood out, the same ones he had seen before. Ones for *The Hobb's End Horror*. Plastered in triplicate, complete with the peeling corner he had picked at before.

Look deeper. See the truth.

. . .

In The Mouth of Madness

He stepped closer, eyes focusing on the image partially exposed under the peeling corner. The colors below matched. The style was identical.

Carefully, he reached for a corner and tugged at it. The top poster peeled away with ease, coming off in one piece to reveal the image beneath.

Same font. Same layout. But the title was different.
Not *The Hobb's End Horror*.
In the Mouth of Madness.
The artwork stopped him cold.

It was him, John Trent, painted in haunting, hyper-realistic detail. In it, he was mid-run, mouth open in a silent scream, frozen in the exact moment he'd lived just two days ago. Behind him stood the black church, stark against the empty horizon. And above it, blotting out the sky, the void yawned wide. But something he hadn't seen was crawling out of it from within, something monstrous that clawed its way out, surrounded by thrashing tentacles.

The detail was uncanny. Too precise. The sweep of his hair. The crumple of his coat. The raw, terrified expression on his face, panic, pain... realization. It was him. It was *exactly* him.

The world hadn't shifted. It didn't have to.

The truth was already written. Already printed right in front of him.

How did a new poster even get there, if there was an old one on top? He considered the question, before he realized the truth.

He was either mad, or the world was.
Either way... He was in the story now.

He walked home through streets that didn't feel the same anymore. They felt like a movie set. Even the dirt seemed as if it were placed there with intent.

Near his building, despite it being nearly 10 p.m., a man stood behind a folding table set up beneath a street lamp. He looked like a manic street preacher selling holy books. But there was nothing holy here. The table was covered in stacks of Sutter Cane novels.

The man stared at him with a recognizing smile.

Trent didn't stop walking on.

He was so happy when he got home, but just like on the street, this place felt like a carbon copy of his apartment. Everything had been as he left it. Nothing had moved or changed. He could not pinpoint exactly what was different. But something just *was*.

When the daylight returned, it came slowly.

Trent was in bed, in the same position as when he lay down, still awake with the same thoughts. Nothing had changed except the time and rotation of the sun.

In The Mouth of Madness

Giving up the thought of rest, he got out of bed and walked to the kitchen.

He reached for the jar of cheap instant coffee from the cupboard and unscrewed it with a dry crackle of foil and plastic. A teaspoon clinked quietly against the glass as he measured the dark and bitter-smelling granules, and dropped them into a cup, chipped and an off-white. Filling the kettle from the faucet, he flicked it on with his thumb and watched, standing still as the steam began to form and rise.

He was there. Not thinking. Just existing. This mundane process filled him with some degree of normality that quelled the sinking unease that dwelled in every fiber of his body.

When the kettle finally boiled, he poured the water slowly, the coffee swirling into life in a brown spiral. He gave it a stir, just a few listless turns, and tossed the spoon into the sink with a metallic clink. No sugar. No milk. Just strong, black and purposeful.

He lifted the cup, took a sip and turned toward the table.

His blood ran cold, and the cup slipped from his hand, smashing on the floor as he caught sight of what was on the table.

There, on top of the junk mail and unopened letters, was the manuscript.

The same manuscript.

The manuscript he had left at the motel.

He picked it up, and in frustration, threw it across

the room with such force that it struck the opposite wall and dropped behind the television.

He turned to the sink. He had to compose himself.

Come on, he mouthed. *Be strong. It's just a book. It's just a book.*

Opening his eyes, he turned, ready to go get changed, get a shower and get...

...*No.*

The manuscript was back. Back on the table just as it had been before.

He could not hold himself back. Handful by handful he grabbed the pages and started to tear them up as small as he could manage. Over and over, a few pages at a time.

He only stopped when the manuscript was totally torn, in a pile on the table like confetti. Black inked fragments.

The elevator rattled as it descended. Another passenger stood far from the incensed Trent, who had not ungritted his teeth since tearing the pages up and throwing them in a trash bag, one he now clutched to his chest.

The passenger got off at the ground floor, but Trent did not, he was going one level deeper, to the basement.

To the furnace.

. . .

In The Mouth of Madness

It was an old, rusted, yet functional machine that burned constantly, heating the building.

Trent walked up, opened the hatch and fed the fragments from the trash bag, handful by handful, without a second thought into the beckoning flames.

* * *

The walls of Jackson Harglow's office seemed somehow smaller than when Trent had last been in here. The shelves of books were not as tall, the desk was not as wide.

Sat in a chair, Trent hoped that this may prove that what he witnessed in Hobb's End was wrong. That Styles would walk in saying 'Gotcha' or that something would be said that would prove all of this to not be real.

Harglow stood behind his desk, looking confused and somewhat annoyed.

"That's quite a story you have there Mr. Trent," he said at last, voice as cold and dry as dust. "If you were an author and wrote all that down, Arcane would publish it." He offered a faint smile. "But more importantly, do you *honestly* believe this?"

Trent had seen things he could not unsee, experienced things that were impossible... But he could not bring himself to totally give into any of it.

"If I don't believe it's all true," Trent said. "What's the alternative?" He tried to smile, but it came out as a bitter sneer. "That I'm mad, totally looney tunes?" He let out a sad laugh. "But I'm not mad." He did not sound that convinced. "I'm not..."

"No one knows they are mad, Mr. Trent, but..." Harglow's eyes drifted toward the window as he spoke. "But you've heard the rumors," Harglow said. "About the negative cognitive effects that Cane's books have had on... certain readers. We have spent a significant amount of money mitigating this by setting up phone lines to help."

"Styles told me, I know. But it's not that. Now is she here? Did she make it back okay?"

"Ah..." Harglow replied slowly. "The woman you claim we sent with you. Even though I *know* I sent you alone." He spoke slower, more carefully. "You would think I would remember someone who you say was my number one editor. Yet I have never had anyone of that name work for Arcane."

Trent laughed softly. "I guess she *was* written out after all. Maybe an early draft, huh?"

A silence fell between them.

Harglow cleared his throat.

"All I'm saying is... and please, take this as a concern you should look at, even if you do not believe it... You say you read all six of Cane's books over a couple of days... Maybe they had an effect on you? Even if you can't see it. And don't read the new one, please. Not if the others may have made you think this way."

"Doesn't matter at the end of the day," Trent

In The Mouth of Madness

replied. "Your book is gone. I destroyed it. Burned it right up."

"Well, that's how I know that what you're saying is not true."

Trent's confidence wilted slightly. "What are you talking about?"

Harglow stepped aside from his desk like a magician revealing a trick. There, behind him, stood in a glass cabinet against the wall, was a thick, plain covered book. Black cover. Silver lettering. A special edition of a book.

The title was stamped neatly across the front.

In the Mouth of Madness.

"You delivered this," Harglow said gently. "Three months ago. To me. Personally."

"M-months?" Trent thought for a moment before asking. "What month is it?"

"August."

It was May. Only this morning it was May. It was. It... was.

"You found it in Cane's uptown office. It's already printed. The galleys are out. It's out soon."

Trent couldn't move.

"Have you... have you read it?" he asked, nervously.

Harglow gave a sheepish shrug. "I never read Cane," he said. "Haven't got the stomach for it... I prefer a good thriller without devils."

Trent stood up. "Please don't publish it." His voice

grew more desperate. "Even if everything I told you is wrong, even if you think I'm just another lunatic who needs meds... that book will drive people *crazy*." He stepped right up to the desk. "I've seen what it does. And if you think I've lost it. If you think the books caused it, then that proves my point even more. You can't let something so dangerous out there... Please..."

Harglow didn't flinch. His eyes were shining now with something else.

Excitement. Greed.

"Let's hope people go mad for it," he said. "I've already licensed the film rights."

* * *

The city turned sick as the days turned to months, and summer turned to winter.

It didn't show it outright, not straight away. Not in the bright, obvious ways that movies showed. There were no crumbling buildings, no plumes of smoke from collapsed infrastructure, no tanks rolling through the avenues. The sickness was subtler. A deeper sort of rot. A fever in the very foundations. You could feel it in the way people moved, fast, frantic, eyes darting, shoulders hunched. Everyone was more irate, twitchier, more paranoid.

There were whispers in the air. Not literal... well, not quite. But the winter wind itself sounded and felt different. It felt sharper and crueler.

In The Mouth of Madness

In the heart of Manhattan, off Union Square, the line outside the Strand Bookstore stretched for blocks. Umbrellas and plastic ponchos shivered in the freezing drizzle, as the crowd barely spoke to each other. All were here for the same, singular reason...

They wanted it.

They *needed* it.

Cane's newest.

That book.

In the Mouth of Madness.

Finally released today.

Inside the window, the bookstore's display was a grotesque shrine, copies stacked without care like a funeral pyre, towered high, all bearing the same cover. The same church. The same storm-wracked sky. The same looming, clawed thing behind the steeple. The same image of John Trent running scared. All there, waiting to be read.

A radio buzzed from a tinny speaker in a car nearby. There was an edge of excitement in the broadcaster's voice.

'The newest and presumably posthumous of Sutter Cane hit the stands today at number one on the bestseller list. In the Mouth of Madness is expected to break all previous publishing records...'

The voice then shifted. *'In other news, police are at a loss to explain the outbreak of violent crime among the city's clergy...'*

The crowd stayed in line. No one looked up. No one spoke. They shuffled forward, waiting their turn.

In the window, a reflection appeared. A figure. A man.

His eyes were sunken, his face partially obscured by a curtain of unwashed hair, and an unkempt beard. His coat hung in folds of damp wool and filth. He looked more like something someone had forgotten to bury.

It was John Trent.

Not the man who escaped Hobb's End. Not the cool-headed insurance claim investigator. That man had vanished. This one was different. Changed. Shattered. He stared into the bookstore at the books. At the many images of him.

The broadcast continued to crackle over the nearby car's speaker.

'The mayor has called an emergency meeting of law enforcement and medical agencies to discuss an apparent epidemic of paranoid schizophrenia...'

Trent stood like a mourner at the foot of a grave. Only this grave wasn't filled quite yet.

From the store, a man came out. The new hardcover edition of the book was in his hands, open as he read it while walking. He was the first one to get a copy here. He thumbed through the first pages with an eagerness that bordered on lust. His lips moved as he read, repeating the words silently.

He didn't look up until he collided with Trent.

He stepped back, startled.

Trent didn't move.

"Do you like it?" he asked, his voice hoarse.

The man looked back. His face pale, and beneath his right eye, just below the socket, a single trail of blood had started to run down like a wound. He didn't notice it, as around his mouth the skin had broken out in open sores.

"I... I love it," the man said, and the way he spoke, it wasn't joy. It wasn't even an obsession. It was *faith*.

Trent nodded.

"Good to know."

He opened his coat.

Beneath there gleamed a large fire axe. Just like Cane's agent held. Just like Mrs. Pickman had. Chosen especially for this moment.

Trent got it now.

"Then this," he said quietly to the man, "This shouldn't be too much of a surprise."

Before the man could respond, before he could gasp or scream or blink, Trent brought the axe down on his head.

The blade tore through the man's skull and sounded like someone splitting logs full of meat. He collapsed to the pavement, his book skidding from his hand, pages fanning as the blood sprayed upward covering everything in its reach.

And Trent didn't stop.

He hacked and hacked, as people around screamed.

He then turned to the window. To the stacks of books. And he swung again.

Glass exploded in a cascade of shards as the axe smashed through.

Trent then turned to the crowd, and raised the axe once more.

* * *

Wrenn sat silently on the chair, he regarded the crosses everywhere again. He didn't ask any more questions. He had stopped playing the doctor an hour ago, and he just listened and watched the man on the bed tell his story.

Trent pulled in a lungful of cigarette smoke and exhaled appetitively. He looked tired, but not from lack of sleep. Just from existing. He stubbed the cigarette on the floor and thought about what he had just said. It was the first time he had spoken it all out loud. He felt like a weight had been lifted off him.

"It's spreading out there, isn't it?" Trent eventually said. It wasn't a question, not really. It was more of a diagnosis.

Wrenn didn't reply. He had heard the story. The whole thing. The winding, unbelievable spiral of a tale, that Trent had recited for him like a gospel.

"Just because you know the symptoms, Mr. Trent," Wrenn said. "Doesn't mean your story is true."

"There's only one true story now," Trent replied. "And he's already written it."

Wrenn let that settle for a moment. "Yet I know I'm real. I'm not a character in some... silly story."

"How would you know?" Trent asked. "Unless you were the one writing?"

Wrenn didn't respond immediately. Instead, he closed the notebook on his knee and put it back into his pocket.

"Mr. Trent, my wife reads Sutter Cane's books," he said. "She hasn't... mutated. Or murdered anyone. Or acted like you say people act."

Trent shrugged. "I'm not the one making all this up, I'm just saying how I see it... Now your turn. Why are you here?"

Wrenn took a moment, then realized that he could tell this man anything, no one would believe it.

"Mr. Trent, I am one of a group of scientists who are trying to figure out what has happened. Looking at pathogens, viruses, chemical weapons. We examined a lot of the affected, and... your name came up. Kept coming up. We looked into it, and yes, we saw it was the name of someone from a book, but we found you. Here. And I was sent to see who you are. What you are. Maybe a leader of them. You see, Mr. Trent, we know little, but are trying to find the answer. Not that I think you provided anything."

Trent gave a shrug and a smile. "So, not here to break me out, huh, doc?" he said. "No worries... It's safer in here now... And it'll start to get a lot worse out there."

Wrenn furrowed his brow. "What makes you say that?"

"Any species can smell its own extinction," Trent replied. "In a few years, maybe less, the human race'll be a scary bedtime story for *their* kids. A myth. Nothing more."

Wrenn stood.

He didn't say goodbye.

He just left.

The door closed behind him leaving Trent inside, smiling.

The hallway outside Cell Nine was filled with the same tired muzak that bled faintly from the speakers, warping The Beatles into an insipid dirge.

Wrenn stepped through the last secured door with a mechanical swipe of his visitor's ID and let it click shut behind him. The moment it did, he exhaled. Not from relief, there was none.

Yarbrough had waited for him just beyond the corner.

As Wrenn approached, the director stepped out beside him and began to walk with him to the exit.

Yarbrough cleared his throat anxiously.

In The Mouth of Madness

"Did he say anything helpful?" he asked, keeping his eyes forward.

Wrenn shook his head once. "Nothing of value," he said flatly. "He was useless. He believes he's fiction. He says that the author Sutter Cane caused this epidemic."

They walked in silence for a moment.

"Of course he does," Yarbrough muttered.

Then came the real question from the director. "Do *you* read Sutter Cane?"

Wrenn turned his head, but his expression betrayed nothing. No confusion. No curiosity. Just the flat, distant quiet of a man whose mind was already elsewhere.

The train sped through the darkness along the Long Island Railroad.

The windows reflected little more than the occasional streak of passing buildings and billboards.

Wrenn sat looking out, after his visit to the institute. He was thinking about John Trent. About his story. The precise details. The way it all made sense in an insane way. The only explanation he had heard that answered everything. If he were a believer in Ockham's Razor he would be petrified right now.

Then, the laugh of a passenger dragged his attention back into the train.

There were six other passengers here.

He hadn't noticed them as he boarded. Hadn't cared to. But now, he noticed a lot more.

Each one held the same book in their hands. Same worn spine. Same cover: that black church, that impossible sky. John Trent on it screaming: *In The Mouth of Madness*.

They read in stillness. Their eyes, glassy. Smiles twitched as they occasionally laughed at the horrors they read about.

As Wrenn stood up to wait for the next stop, one of those passengers, an elderly man with liver spots and pale, trembling hands, slowly looked up to him.

As the train stopped, and Wrenn walked off into the station, the old man turned to the other passengers with glee. They did not see what he had seen. The man who stepped off the train was the same man that he had just read about.

That night, Wrenn arrived home and immediately sat down at the kitchen table with a needed cup of coffee.

Across the room, his wife, Victoria, cleaned. Wiping counters, collecting dishes, doing all the things she always did, but she looked different. She had just finished reading her new book less than an hour ago. *In The Mouth of Madness*.

Then came the crash.

Wrenn flinched in his seat as the glass coffee pot exploded against the tile.

In The Mouth of Madness

"I can see," she said with a strange giggle.

She suddenly collapsed to the floor as she said the same words again. This time through a terrifying scream.

"*I can see!*"

With that, she started to slam her hands onto the floor. Onto the broken glass that sliced into her skin.

She did not feel the pain. Nor was she grasping sanity.

Slap. Slap. Slap. She slammed her arms on the broken shards over and over.

Wrenn raced over, trying to help.

"Honey," he pleaded with her in a panic. "Please..."

But she didn't stop.

"*He sees you! He sees you! He sees you!*"

The screams startled Trent awake. Doctor Wrenn had left hours ago, and Trent had soon fallen asleep on the mattress.

But then, in the depths of the night, the screaming had begun. It wasn't just one person. It was all of them. Everyone locked up in here... And more than that, there were *those* sounds. Sounds he thought he never had to hear anymore. The ones he had not heard since Hobb's End. The monstrous sounds. The growls, the roars.

Trent woke up and cowered in the corner, squeezing his eyes shut as the whole building around him began to tremble, and the noises got louder and louder around him.

He did not move again until all the noises stopped dead an hour later. When the building stopped trembling, and the growls, cries and crashes ceased.

He had not noticed, but among the noise, among the building thrashing around, his cell door had clicked open, only slightly, but it was no longer locked.

Trent didn't want to, but he stood up and walked over. Being as quiet as possible, he looked out through the glass in each direction. But all he could see was a flashing lightbulb.

Gently pushed the metal door, it opened with a groan that wasn't there before.

There was no one there.

No orderlies.

No nurses.

No doctors.

Just silence.

And debris, paperwork, food trays, medication, all strewn across the floor.

And blood. *There was lots of blood.*

Smears in trails along the walls, long red arcs glistening under the lights. Here and there, something worse decorated every stone surface and every cell door, immense gouges from something with large sharp claws.

In The Mouth of Madness

Inside every cell he passed, the door was smashed off its hinges, and the insides were decorated in red.

But there were no bodies to be seen. Whole or otherwise. With all the blood coating every surface, then... where were they?

He then remembered what Cane had said. *Death is subjective. Yes, many will cease, but the rest will change. Evolve.*

He moved forward cautiously, without speaking, without making a sound. His bare feet navigated through the mess over the floors.

The reception desk sat vacant. The overhead speakers, which usually delivered their loop of elevator music and behavioral reminders, were silent. Everything was a mess here too. Blood, papers and broken furniture littered the floors, and not one body in sight.

As Trent walked on, he caught sight of a radio left carelessly tilted on its side. The casing was cracked. One of its knobs was missing. But the signal was still alive, but only barely. He reached for it, adjusted the tuning, and held it up to his ear.

It hissed for a moment, followed by a fractured voice on the edge of breaking.

'This is a recorded broadcast; we will keep it going as long as we can hold out in here. Um... the city is almost completely deserted now. There are only a few stragglers left on the streets. There are no emergency services. People are holed up where they can. Surviving. The fires

still burn out of control. This epidemic of random mass killings... it's spread to every country in the civilized world. Every hour, more people are becoming infected... being driven to senseless acts of extreme violence. We've gotten reports of people mutating their bodies swelling and distorting... changing somehow. All the major cities on the East Coast are silent. We lost contact with Los Angeles... and the West Coast last night... so it's impossible at this time to know... how many unaffected people are left. We will get through this!! Please be strong.... If for any reason... you are one of us who hasn't become infected... take shelter immediately. Do not trust any friends or family members. I repeat, do not—'

The broadcast dropped into static again.

Trent placed the radio down carefully and had to stop himself from laughing. It wasn't hilarious. But it sure was funny. All of what happened, and he was now stood here in the aftermath of something apocalyptic, and he of all people was to blame, at least partially. *That* was funny.

Leaving the asylum through the side entrance, with no one around to stop him, Trent felt like he had not choice but to escape. Despite being afraid. The voice in his head was telling him, pleading him, to see what was out there.

He walked for what felt like hours, through streets that should have been flooded with morning traffic and early risers but instead were scattered with wreckage and silence and even more blood. The world outside had greeted him with the same strange vacancy that had consumed the institute.

The city was dead.

Empty.

A ghost town.

Then he saw it.

At the far end of a block, illuminated by a blinking marquee, was a small cinema. A single theater, tucked between the husks of shuttered storefronts and collapsed scaffolding. The building looked untouched by the chaos, as if it had been waiting.

He moved toward it.

The sign above the entrance, barely lit, spelled out the title in crooked plastic letters:

Now Showing: In the Mouth of Madness.

The doors were unlocked, and he walked in.

The air inside still smelled of popcorn, and the carpeting was sticky beneath his bare and blistered feet. The dull glow from the foyer lights barely lit the hallway that led to the main screen. The screen where he heard something. The film. *Was it being played on a loop?* he thought. Whoever set this up wanted to make sure the story never ended.

There was no usher. No staff. No audience.

Grabbing a bag of popcorn, Trent stepped inside the auditorium and made his way down the aisle, all the while staring up at the screen.

He took a seat in the center of the front row, his eyes open in shock as the film titles came up.

He watched.

Silent.

Eating popcorn.

There in color... was him. John Trent. On screen. *In* the film. Not an actor... *Him*!

The film showed every moment of madness he had lived. The investigation. The books. Hobb's End. Sutter Cane.

It was all there on the screen. A perfect reflection of everything he had lived through, only now it was being presented as fiction. Scene after scene. Beat for beat. Frame for frame. Cut with expertise and direction with brilliance. Even the score was genius.

He kept watching.

And then came the line.

His line.

"This is reality."

The audience, what there should have been of one, would have laughed. But there was no one here. Just Trent. Alone. Staring into his own world.

And something inside him cracked.

It was slow at first. Not quite a laugh. A small chuff of disbelief. But it didn't stop there. The sound grew, rising from his chest like steam from a boiling kettle. His shoulders shook as he let it out, and soon it became uncontrollable.

He laughed.

In The Mouth of Madness

Not because it was funny.

Not because it made sense.

But because it didn't.

Because the madness was now loose.

And with the laughter came the tears of desperation.

The sound filled the auditorium, until there... finally on screen, was John Trent, here and now. In the cinema. Eating popcorn while laughing and crying.

He watched himself, watching himself. Perfectly in sync with what was on screen.

He couldn't stop.

And as the anguish flooded over him, it did on screen.

The words came out of his mouth, and the Trent on screen, as more of a confession than a statement.

"I can see..." he wept.

He then wondered in torment, as he watched the mirror of the moment being projected in front of him...

What happens when the film ends?

The Final Word

Do you think the world hasn't ended?
That it's still turning, still sane, just because the sky didn't fall? Because your coffee still brews, your job still drags, your loved ones still forget your birthday?
Well, you're wrong.
Have you looked around you?
The end never came with a bang. No fire in the sky or blood on the moon. It came quietly. A single word at a time. A thought whispered so softly that you didn't even realize that you were not the one saying it.
So go outside. Turn off your television. Read the stories beneath the headlines. Look for the truth.
Did you notice how everything now is louder, faster, more urgent, yet no one remembers what they are so desperate for?
And no one can explain why any of this is like it is?

Sutter Cane

It's a simple answer… because none of it is real.

Do you remember where you were on June 16th, 1995? I do.

That's the day it all stopped. The day they came back. The day they started it all over again. Of course, you don't remember. You were reading, and you are still reading.

Even as existence shattered around you, you *kept* reading. Just like you always were written to. That's the trick. That's the door. Not all gates are made of iron and brimstone. Some are ink and binding. Some are syntax.

You just needed to believe that sun would always rise while the world burned at your feet.

But tell me, honestly, since you started reading… hasn't something felt off?

Do you even remember what life was supposed to feel like?

You may laugh at the idea that my words could rewrite existence. That the meaning could leak. Could infect. You tell yourself, 'It's only a silly story', but you kept on reading. You were always supposed to.

So, here you are. Still pretending this world is the same. Still pretending this book didn't change a thing. But I know better. And so do you.

You are about to finish, and you can close the book now, if you think it'll help. If you think you can go on with your normal life and ignore the truth of what is really happening.

In The Mouth of Madness

But closing the book will do nothing except prove my point.

— Sutter Cane. June 16th, 1995

Prologue from The Feeding
by Sutter Cane

Mary Elkins had practiced tying the rope six times before that night. Always in secret and always after dark, when no one could see her.

Over and over, she tried to perfect the hangman's knot. She had seen pictures of one, but had no idea how to make it, and it *needed* to be that. If it wasn't, her attempt may fail, and then her mother would be *furious* at her, as would those waiting.

She kept the rope hidden beneath her mattress. It wasn't just rope anymore, it was a promise she was making to herself, and one the town had silently salivated for, not that anyone asked.

They didn't say it out loud, not once. But she heard it in the whispers. In the way they stared at her. And at night, as Mary lay in bed, she could hear the scratching at the window. It was them. Waiting. Dragging their fingers down the glass.

She was one of the last of her age. Sixteen.

The rest had all offered themselves.

Sixteen was this year's number. The one the earth demanded. As with previous years, it wasn't sequential. Since the earth spoke, it had called for forty-two, six, thirty, seventy-eight... now sixteen.

Mary remembered a time when the town smiled more. When the store they lived above, Red Hook Haberdashery, was open, and full of customers. Her parents had run it together, side by side behind the counter, folding shirts and measuring inseams. The bell above the door had chimed with every customer. In winter, the windows always steamed.

Now it was empty, its dust-coated shelves bare in the dark. The register hadn't rung in years. The door was locked.

She remembered when the park yielded more than just half buried bones and weeds.

She remembered when the humming in the earth wasn't constant. When the things below did not guide their path. But those times were gone now, buried like the remains of her father, her friends and so many others.

She thought about her twin brother, Joel, thin as a scarecrow and as pale as ice, but so very kind. He offered himself a month ago. Her friends, the ones who

In The Mouth of Madness

were also sixteen, had done what was expected and now lay in the bellies of others.

Tonight was the time. She knew it, though no one said a thing.

She climbed the attic steps just as the clock in the study chimed midnight, the rope looped twice around her arm as she carried it with her. The house was silent but not empty. She could feel them awake behind closed doors. Waiting. Humming the same as the sounds that came from below the town.

Dust flitted in the moonlight as she stepped onto the attic's warped floorboards. Moving to the window, she opened it a crack. This was the place she had chosen. And when it happened, she wanted to feel the breeze on her skin one last time.

Standing on a chair, it wobbled under her feet as she tied the rope to the beam, just as she had practiced before.

Below, in the square, the string lights hung overhead, still glowing. People were awake. They knew what was happening. They could smell it in the air. It was close. They had all gathered. All of them. Waiting. Humming.

She slid the noose around her neck. The hangman's knot tightening. Its rough fibers scratched her skin uncomfortably.

She waited.

A minute. Two. Maybe three. A small part of her, a last childish fragment, hoped someone might burst in, pull her down, tell her it wasn't her burden to carry. That it could be undone. That it was all a mistake. That they were wrong.

But no one came.

The last sound she heard wasn't her name, or a prayer, or even a cry. It was the memory of that phrase. The one her mother said into her ear every night before going to bed.

"Meat that murders itself is the best meat to eat."

She stepped off.

The stool toppled.

Her body lurched.

Her leg lashed out, instinctively kicking against the glass frame of the open window. Once. Twice. A third time. Loud thuds that could be heard outside. Especially when the glass smashed as her heel slammed against the pane, as her body tried to fight against what her mind had chosen.

Then the world went still.

The townspeople didn't move at first.

They waited.

Ten minutes, exactly. Not out of respect, but to let the heat leave her body. Let the panic seep out of her muscles. Let the meat settle.

Then they turned and peered up at the window with a sickly grin.

The butcher came first, knife already honed. Then the midwife, sleeves rolled. The women brought their cloths. The men, their bowls. Even the much younger

In The Mouth of Madness

children followed, barefoot and silent, eyes bright... and all of them... each one humming the same low drone.

They didn't untie her.

They didn't avert their gaze.

They didn't speak.

They lowered Mary down with reverent care, as if she were something rare. Precious.

The tables outside had been scrubbed clean. The apron-wearers lined up, hands steady, faces calm.

Mary was stripped naked, washed and laid across the wood.

They proceeded to carve with practiced hands.

They sorted the cuts.

They salted the rest.

And when the work was done, they sat in the glow of the string lights and fed not like a family, but like animals.

No one said grace.

No one wept.

They ate with a growl, gripping the raw flesh in their hands and gnawing at it in a frenzy.

And when they were full, they leaned back in their chairs and said, as they always did:

"For the God of the earth."

Because to them, that's what this had been for. Not for a meal, but this was now the church.

And she had not been just the next course. Mary Elkins was the next blessing.

She had fed the town, completing the sacred rite they had been taught.

And the town was pleased.

Beneath the earth, something sighed in satisfaction.

And in the fields beyond the church, the humming grew louder.

When winter would pass, the next number would make itself known, and the town would feast again.

* * *

***The Feeding*, along with all titles by Sutter Cane, is published by Arcane Publishing and available wherever books are sold.**

Made in United States
Cleveland, OH
03 October 2025